William Shakespeare, Henry Norman Hudson

Plays of Shakespeare: Selected and Prepared for Use in Schools

Antigonos

William Shakespeare, Henry Norman Hudson

Plays of Shakespeare: Selected and Prepared for Use in Schools

Reprint of the original, first published in 1879.

1st Edition 2024 | ISBN: 978-3-38801-267-4

Antigonos Verlag is an imprint of Outlook Verlagsgesellschaft mbH.

Verlag (Publisher): Outlook Verlag GmbH, Zeilweg 44, 60439 Frankfurt, Deutschland, info@outlook-verlag.de
Vertretungsberechtigt (Authorized to represent): E. Roepke, Zeilweg 44, 60439 Frankfurt, Deutschland
Druck (Print): Libri Plureos GmbH, Friedensallee 273, 22763 Hamburg, Deutschland

PLAYS

OF

SHAKESPEARE

SELECTED AND PREPARED FOR USE IN

SCHOOLS.

WITH INTRODUCTIONS AND NOTES.

BY

THE REV. HENRY N. HUDSON.

NUMBER IV.

THE TEMPEST.

BOSTON:
GINN AND HEATH.
1879.

INTRODUCTION TO THE TEMPEST.

THE TEMPEST was first printed in the folio of 1623, where, for reasons unknown to us, it stands the first in the volume. In regard to the text there are no very serious difficulties, and but a few points that are much disputed. These are remarked in the notes, and so need not be mentioned here.

It is beyond question that this play was among the latest of the Poet's writing. Malone ascertained from some old records that *The Tempest* was acted by the King's players "before Prince Charles, the Princess Elizabeth, and the Prince Palatine, in the beginning of 1613." This is the only authentic contemporary notice we have to help us towards the date of the writing. I say the only *authentic* notice; for the memorandum put forth some years ago by Mr. Cunningham, purporting to be from "Accounts of the Revels at Court," and stating the play to have been acted at Whitehall, November 1, 1611, has been lately discredited. A passage from Florio's translation of Montaigne's *Essays*, quoted in note 17, Act ii. scene 1, shows conclusively that the play must have been written after 1603. But the time of writing is to be gathered more nearly from another source. The play has several points clearly connecting with some of the then recent marvels of Transatlantic discovery; in fact, I suspect America may justly claim to have borne a considerable part in suggesting and shaping this delectable workmanship. In May, 1609, Sir George Somers, with a fleet of nine ships, headed by the *Sea Venture*, which was called the *Admiral's Ship*, sailed for Virginia. In mid-ocean they were struck by a terrible tempest, which scattered the whole fleet; seven of the ships, however, reached Virginia; but the *Sea Venture* was parted from the rest, driven out of her course, and finally wrecked on one of the Bermudas. These islands were then thought to be "a most prodigious and enchanted place, affording nothing but gusts, storms, and foul weather"; on which account they had acquired a bad name. In 1610 appeared a pamphlet entitled *A Discovery of the Bermudas, otherwise called the Isle of Devils*, giving an account of the storm and shipwreck. The sailors had worked themselves into complete exhaustion, and given over in despair, and taken leave of each other, when the ship was found to be jammed in between two rocks, so that all came safe to land. They found the island uninhabited, the air mild and wholesome, the land exceedingly fruitful; "all the fairies of the rocks were but flocks of birds, and all the devils that haunted the woods were but herds of swine." Staying there some nine months they had a very delightful time of it, refitted their ship, and then put to sea again, with an ample supply of provisions, and their minds richly freighted with the beauties and wonders of the place.

There can be no rational doubt that from this narrative Shakespeare took various hints for the matter and whereabout of his drama. Thus much is plainly indicated by his mention of "the still-vexed Bermoothes," as the Bermudas were then called, and also by the qualities of air and soil ascribed to his happy island. It is not to be supposed, however, that the scene of the play lies in the Bermudas; for in less than an hour after the tempest the rest of the fleet is said to be on the Mediterranean, "bound sadly home for Naples." As to the actual scene of the play, this is not easy to determine. Mr. Hunter thinks the Poet had in view the island of Lampedusa, "which lies midway between Malta and the African coast." It may be so; but I rather think the Poet fixed his scene upon an island of the mind; and that he transferred to his ideal whereabout some of the marvels described in the forecited narrative. The supernatural of the play was no doubt Shakespeare's own creation; but it would have been in accordance with his usual method to avail himself of whatever interest might spring from the popular notions touching the Bermudas; and at that time the English people had their imaginations kindled to the highest pitch with marvellous tales of the newly-discovered world.

No play, tale, novel, or writing of any kind has been found which could have furnished any thing towards the plot or characters of *The Tempest*. So that in this respect we can but regard the whole as having been carved fresh out of the Poet's own ideal stock.

The points already stated infer the play to have been written as late as 1610. This inference is fully sustained by the internal evidence of the play itself. Coleridge sets it down as "certainly one of Shakespeare's latest works, judging from the language only." The play has indeed the same peculiarities of workmanship, and these too in their clearest form, which mark the other dramas of his closing period; the style, the versification, the general cast of thought, the union of richness and severity, the grave, austere beauty of character which pervades it, and the organic compactness of the whole structure, all concurring to identify it as an issue of the Poet's ripest years.

The Tempest is on all hands regarded as one of Shakespeare's perfectest works. Some of his plays, I should say, have beams in their eyes, but this has hardly so much as a mote; or, if it has any, my own eyes are not clear enough to discern it. Miranda, Ariel, and Caliban are three of the most unique and original conceptions that ever sprang from the wit of man. We can scarcely imagine how the Ideal could be pushed further beyond Nature; yet we here find it clothed with all the truth and life of Nature. And the whole texture of incident and circumstance is framed in keeping with that Ideal; so that all the parts and particulars cohere together, mutually supporting and supported.

Accordingly the Poet's critics are almost, if not altogether, unanimous in praise of this drama; and the best of them have put forth their best forces of judgment and eloquence in approving and discoursing its beauties. For the purpose here intended, I deem it better to reproduce some of their sayings than to occupy the space with critical remarks of my own. The precious notes which we have from Coleridge are unusually full upon this play. I therefore quote somewhat largely from him:

"The romance opens with a busy scene admirably appropriate to the kind of drama, and giving, as it were, the key-note of the whole harmony. It prepares and initiates the excitement required for the entire piece, and yet does not demand any thing from the spectators which their previous habits had not fitted them to understand. It is the bustle of a tempest, from which the real horrors are abstracted; therefore it is poetical, though not in strictness natural, and is purposely restrained from concentrating the interest on itself, and used merely as an induction or tuning for what is to follow.

"In the second scene, Prospero's speeches, till the entrance of Ariel, contain the finest example I remember of retrospective narration for the purpose of exciting immediate interest, and putting the audience in possession of all the information necessary for the understanding of the plot. Observe, too, the perfect probability of the moment chosen by Prospero to open out the truth to his daughter, his own romantic bearing, and how completely any thing that might have been disagreeable to us in the magician is reconciled and shaded in the humanity and natural feelings of the father. In the very first speech of Miranda the simplicity and tenderness of her character are at once laid open; it would have been lost in direct contact with the agitation of the first scene.

"The appearance and characters of the super- or ultra-natural servants are finely contrasted. Ariel has in every thing the airy tint which gives the name; and it is worthy of remark that Miranda is never directly brought into comparison with Ariel, lest the natural and human of the one and the supernatural of the other should tend to neutralize each other. Caliban, on the other hand, is all earth, all condensed and gross in feelings and images; he has the dawnings of understanding, without reason or the moral sense; and in him, as in some brute animals, this advance to the intellectual faculties, without the moral sense, is marked by the appearance of vice. For it is in the primacy of the moral being only that man is truly human; in his intellectual powers he is certainly approached by the brutes; and, man's whole system duly considered, those powers cannot be viewed as other than means to an end, that is, morality.

"In this scene, as it proceeds, is displayed the impression made by Ferdinand and Miranda on each other; it is love at first sight, — 'at the first sight they have chang'd eyes.' Prospero's interruption of the courtship has often seemed to me to have no sufficient motive; still, his alleged reason — 'lest too light winning make the prize light' — is enough for the ethereal connections of the romantic imagination, although it would not be so for the historical. The whole courting-scene indeed, in the beginning of the third Act, between the lovers, is a masterpiece; and the first dawn of disobedience in the mind of Miranda to the command of her father is very finely drawn, so as to seem the working of the Scriptural command, *Thou shalt leave father and mother*, &c. O, with what exquisite purity this scene is conceived and executed! Shakespeare may sometimes be gross, but I boldly say that he is always moral and modest. Alas! in this our day, decency of manners is preserved at the expense of morality of heart, and delicacies for vice are allowed, whilst grossness against it is hypocritically, or at least morbidly, condemned.

"In this play are admirably sketched the vices generally accompanying a low degree of civilization; and in the first scene of the second Act Shakespeare has, as in many other places, shown the tendency in bad men to indulge in scorn and contemptuous expressions, as a mode of getting rid of their own uneasy feelings of inferiority to the good, and also, by making the good ridiculous, of rendering the transition of others to wickedness easy. Shakespeare never puts habitual scorn into the mouths of other than bad men, as here in the instances of Antonio and Sebastian. Observe how the effect of this scene is heightened by contrast with another counterpart of it in low life, — that between the conspirators Stephano, Caliban, and Trinculo, in the second scene of the third Act, in which there are the same essential characteristics."

Heraud's *Inner Life of Shakespeare* gives the following singular and highly original view of Prospero: "A will, to be perfectly free, must act purely in a moral sphere, where will and power are one. This privilege can rarely be shared by the man of action, who, though he may shape many things according to his wish, must find in his experience much intractable matter that defies alteration. It belongs more especially to the contemplative man, who, whether sa e, poet, or artist, acts in a spiritual sphere, where all is pliant to voluntary action, and to desire is to possess. Here it is possible to create a world in the image of its producer, and fill it with agents who play the parts which he had designed in the manner that he had appointed. Here the soul communicates with higher powers, and receives inspirations and revelations not granted to the lower faculties and organs that operate in the fields of sensible and animal experience. Here it expatiates in dreams of a past or future Paradise. Such a contemplatist is Prospero, — a lofty and serenely minded man, whose soul breathes the pure air of conscience, and lives on angels' food. And what if in him we may see ' the very Shakespeare himself, as it were, of the tempest ?' Such is Coleridge's remark ; and it contains, I think, more truth than he meant to convey. If in any character that he has drawn, Shakespeare has certainly portrayed himself in this."

I must also quote a happy passage touching the heroine from Gervinus, the distinguished German critic : " Miranda is one of those exquisite feminine creations of the Poet, whose excellence does not depend on peculiar prominent qualities, but on that tranquil harmony and purity which we feel to be so agreeable and desirable in women ; like Cordelia, Ophelia, Perdita, she is one of those quiet natures, whose mental worth is closed as within a bud, whose depth of character is hidden, till the occasion comes and reveals the richness of the inner life. Reared in solitude, she is like a blank leaf as regards all social gifts and conventional accomplishments ; but her fancy is full of inward life and playfulness, and her pure soul uninjured by intercourse with mankind. She could acquire few faults and few virtues, as opportunity for both was wanting. Thus the Poet endowed her with modesty and pity, virtues that may be acquired in solitude, and that form a soil in which every other virtue may be planted."

Schlegel gives much the same view of Caliban as that already quoted from Coleridge ; describing him as " a mixture of gnome and savage, half-demon, half-brute, in whose behaviour we perceive at once the traces of his native disposition and the influence of Prospero's education " ; and finally comparing his mind to a dark cave, into which the light of knowledge falling neither illuminates nor warms it, but only serves to put in motion the poisonous vapours generated there. And in reference to him and Ariel he adds the following : " They are neither of them simple allegorical personifications, but beings individually determined. In general we find, in *A Midsummer-Night's Dream*, in *The Tempest*, in the magical part of *Macbeth* and wherever Shakespeare avails himself of the popular belief in the invisible presence of spirits, and the possibility of coming in contact with them, a profound view of the inward life of Nature, and her mysterious springs, which, it is true, can never be altogether unknown to the genuine poet, but which few have possessed in an equal degree with Dante and himself."

The comic portions and characters of this play are in Shakespeare's raciest vein ; yet they are perfectly unique and singular withal, being quite unlike any other of his preparations in that kind, as much so as if they were the growth of a different planet.

THE TEMPEST.

PERSONS REPRESENTED.

ALONSO, King of Naples.
SEBASTIAN, his Brother.
PROSPERO, the rightful Duke of Milan.
ANTONIO, his Brother, the usurping Duke of Milan.
FERDINAND, Son to the King of Naples.
GONZALO, an honest old Counsellor of Naples.
ADRIAN,
FRANCISCO, } Lords.
CALIBAN, a savage and deformed Slave
TRINCULO, a Jester.

STEPHANO, a drunken Butler.
Master of a Ship, Boatswain, and Mariners.

MIRANDA, Daughter to Prospero.

ARIEL, an airy Spirit.
IRIS,
CERES,
JUNO, } presented by Spirits.
Nymphs,
Reapers,

Other Spirits attending on Prospero.

SCENE, the Sea, with a Ship; afterwards an uninhabited Island.

ACT I. SCENE I. *On a Ship at Sea. A Storm, with Thunder and Lightning.*

Enter Master and Boatswain severally.

Mast. Boatswain!
Boats. Here, Master: what cheer?
Mast. Good, speak to the mariners:[1] fall to't yarely, or we run ourselves aground: bestir, bestir. [*Exit.*

Enter Mariners.

Boats. Heigh, my hearts! cheerly, cheerly, my hearts! yare, yare![2] Take in the topsail! tend to the Master's whistle. [*Exeunt Mariners.*]— Blow till thou burst thy wind, if room enough.

Enter ALONSO, SEBASTIAN, ANTONIO, FERDINAND, GONZALO, *and others.*

Alon. Good Boatswain, have care. Where's the Master? Play the men.[3]

---

1 This has been commonly printed with a (:) after *Good;* thus making the sense to be "good *cheer,*" which is certainly wrong. *Good* means "good *friend*" or "good *fellow,*" as twice afterwards in this scene: "Nay, *good,* be patient."

2 *Yare* is here an imperative verb,—be *nimble,* be *quick,* or *active.* The word is seldom if ever used now in any form, but was much used in the Poet's time. In North's *Plutarch* we have such phrases as "galleys not *yare* of steerage," and "ships light of *yarage,*" and "galleys heavy of *yarage.*" *If room enough* means *if we have sea-room enough.*

3 Act with spirit, behave like men. So, in 2 *Samuel* x. 12: "Be of good courage, and let us *play the men* for our people."

1 *

Boats. I pray now, keep below.

Ant. Where 's the Master, Boatswain ?

Boats. Do you not hear him ? You mar our labour: keep your cabins ; you do assist the storm.

Gon. Nay, good, be patient.

Boats. When the sea is. Hence ! What care these roarers for the name of king ? To cabin : silence ! trouble us not.

Gon. Good, yet remember whom thou hast aboard.

Boats. None that I more love than myself. You are a counsellor : if you can command these elements to silence, and work the peace of the present, we will not hand a rope more ; use your authority : if you cannot, give thanks you have liv'd so long, and make yourself ready in your cabin for the mischance of the hour, if it so hap. — Cheerly, good hearts ! — Out of our way, I say.

                                [*Exit.*

Gon. I have great comfort from this fellow : methinks he hath no drowning-mark upon him ; his complexion is perfect gallows. Stand fast, good Fate, to his hanging ! make the rope of his destiny our cable, for our own doth little advantage ! If he be not born to be hang'd, our case is miserable.   [*Exeunt.*

Re-enter Boatswain.

Boats. Down with the top-mast ![4] yare ; lower, lower ! Bring her to : try with main-course.[5] [*A Cry within.*] A plague upon this howling ! they are louder than the weather or our office. —

Re-enter SEBASTIAN, ANTONIO, *and* GONZALO.

Yet again ! what do you here ? Shall we give o'er, and drown ? Have you a mind to sink ?

Seb. A pox o' your throat, you bawling, blasphemous, uncharitable dog !

Boats. Work you, then.

Ant. Hang, cur, hang ! you insolent noise-maker, we are less afraid to be drown'd than thou art.

---

4 Of this order Lord Mulgrave, a sailor critic, says: "The striking the top-mast was a new invention in Shakespeare's time, which he here very properly introduces. He has placed his ship in the situation in which it was indisputably right to strike the top-mast, — where he had not sea-room."

5 I follow Mr. White's punctuation here; which, he says, was suggested to him by Mr. William Story, of Boston. The passage is commonly printed, "Bring her *to try* with main-course." In support of his pointing Mr. White aptly quotes from Lord Mulgrave's comments on this scene: "The gale increasing, the top-mast is struck, to take the weight from aloft, make the ship drive less to leeward, and bear the mainsail, under which the ship is *brought to.*"

Gon. I'll warrant him for drowning,[6] though the ship were no stronger than a nut-shell.

Boats. Lay her a-hold, a-hold! set her two courses![7] off to sea again; lay her off!

Re-enter Mariners, wet.

Mar. All lost! to prayers, to prayers! all lost!
            [Exeunt.

Boats. What, must our mouths be cold?

Gon. The King and Prince at prayers! let us assist them,
For our case is as theirs.

Seb.   I'm out of patience.

Ant. We're merely[8] cheated out of our lives by drunkards.
This wide-chapp'd rascal, — would thou might'st lie drowning,
The washing of ten tides!

Gon.   He'll be hang'd yet,
Though every drop of water swear against it,
And gape at wid'st to glut him.[9]

A confused Noise within. Mercy on us! We split, we split! — Farewell, my wife and children! — Farewell, brother! — We split, we split, we split! [*Exit Boatswain.*

Ant. Let's all sink with the King.   [*Exit.*

Seb. Let's take leave of him.   [*Exit.*

Gon. Now would I give a thousand furlongs of sea for an acre of barren ground; ling, heath, broom, furze, any thing.[10] The wills above be done! but I would fain die a dry death.[11]   [*Exit.*

---

[6] "*For* drowning" is the same in sense as "*from* drowning"; in accordance with old usage. Gonzalo is speaking on the strength of the old proverb, "He that is born to be hanged will never be drowned."

[7] A ship's *courses* are her largest lower sails; "so called," says Holt, "because they contribute most to give her way through the water, and thus enable her to feel the helm, and steer her *course* better than when they are not *set* or spread to the wind." Captain Glascock, another sailor critic, comments thus: "The ship's head is to be put leeward, and the vessel to be drawn off the land under that canvas nautically denominated the two courses." To *lay a ship a-hold* is to bring her to lie as near the wind as she can, in order to keep clear of the land, and get her out to sea.

[8] *Merely* is *entirely, absolutely;* a Latinism. See vol. i. page 527, note 18.

[9] To *englut,* to *swallow* him.

[10] *Ling, heath, broom,* and *furze* were names of plants growing on British barrens. So in Harrison's description of Britain, prefixed to *Holinshed:* "*Brome, heth, firze,* brakes, whinnes, *ling,* &c." The original has *long heath, brown furze;* but there is no vegetation known that was or could properly be so named. The reading in the text is approved by Walker and adopted by Dyce.

[11] Lord Mulgrave thinks Shakespeare must have conversed with some of the best seamen of the time, as "no books had then been published on the

Scene II. *The Island : before the Cell of* Prospero.

Enter Prospero *and* Miranda.

Mira. If by your art, my dearest father, you have
Put the wild waters in this roar, allay them.
The sky, it seems, would pour down stinking pitch,
But that the sea, mounting to th'[1] welkin's cheek,
Dashes the fire out. O, I have suffer'd
With those that I saw suffer ! a brave vessel,
Who had no doubt some noble creatures in her
Dash'd all to pieces. O, the cry did knock
Against my very heart ! Poor souls, they perish'd '
Had I been any god of power, I would
Have sunk the sea within the earth, or e'er[2]
It should the good ship so have swallow'd, and
The fraughting souls within her.
  Pros.   Be collected;
No more amazement : tell your piteous heart
There's no harm done.
  Mira.   O, woe the day !
  Pros.   No harm.
I have done nothing but in care of thee, —
Of thee, my dear one, thee, my daughter, — who
Art ignorant of what thou art, nought knowing
Of whence I am ; nor that I am more better
Than Prospero, master of a full poor cell,
And thy no greater father.
  Mira.   More to know
Did never meddle with my thoughts.[3]
  Pros.   'Tis time
I should inform thee further. Lend thy hand,
And pluck my magic garment from me. — So :
        [*Lays down his Robe.*
Lie there, my art.[4] — Wipe thou thine eyes ; have comfort.

su...ject." He then exhibits the ship in five positions, and shows how truly
these are represented by the words of the dialogue, and says : " The succession of events is strictly observed in the natural progress of the distress
described. the expedients adopted are the best that could have been devised
for a chance of safety : the words of command are not only strictly proper,
but are only such as point to the object to be attained, and no superfluous
ones of detail."

[1] The Poet very often, especially in his later plays, thus shortens *the*, and
so makes it coalesce with the preceding word into one syllable. The
original has many such instances in this play. Here *to th'* makes one syllable. So, later in this scene : " Confederates *wi' th'* King of Naples."

[2] *Before, sooner than ;* as in *Ecclesiastes,* " *or ever* the silver cord be
loosed."

[3] To *meddle,* is to *mix,* or *mingle* with.

[4] So in Fuller's *Holy State :* " Lord Burghley, at night when he put off

The direful spectacle o' the wreck, which touch'd
The very virtue of compassion in thee,
I have with such prevision in mine art
So safely order'd, that there is no soul —
No, not so much perdition as an hair,
Betid to any creature in the vessel
Which thou heard'st cry, which thou saw'st sink. Sit
        down;
For thou must now know further.
   Mira.   You have often
Begun to tell me what I am; but stopp'd,
And left me to a bootless inquisition,
Concluding, *Stay, not yet.*
   Pros.   The hour's now come;
The very minute bids thee ope thine ear:
Obey, and be attentive. Canst thou remember
A time before we came unto this cell?
I do not think thou canst; for then thou wast not
Out three years old.[5]
   Mira.   Certainly, sir, I can.
   Pros. By what? by any other house or person?
Of any thing the image tell me, that
Hath kept with thy remembrance.
   Mira.   'Tis far off,
And rather like a dream than an assurance
That my remembrance warrants. Had I not
Four or five women once that tended me?
   Pros. Thou hadst, and more, Miranda. But how is't
That this lives in thy mind? What seest thou else
In the dark backward and abysm of time?[6]
If thou remember'st aught ere thou cam'st here,
How thou cam'st here, thou may'st.[7]
   Mira.   But that I do not.
   Pros. Twelve year since,[8] Miranda, twelve year since,
Thy father was the Duke of Milan, and
A prince of power.
   Mira.   Sir, are not you my father?
   Pros. Thy mother was a piece of virtue, and
She said thou wast my daughter; and thy father

his gown, used to say, 'Lie there, Lord Treasurer'; and, bidding adieu to
all State affairs, disposed himself to his quiet rest."
   [5] Not *full*, not *quite* three years old. The Poet has elsewhere a like use
of *out.*
   [6] *Abysm* was the old mode of spelling *abyss*; from the French *abisme.*
   [7] If thou remember'st aught *ere* cam'st here, thou mayst also remember
how thou cam'st here.
   [8] Shakespeare often thus uses the singular form with a plural sense, especially in words denoting time and space.

Was Duke of Milan ; thou his only heir,
A princess, — no worse issu'd.
    Mira.   O the Heavens!
What foul play had we, that we came from thence?
Or blessed was 't we did ?
    Pros.   Both, both, my girl :
By foul play, as thou say'st, were we heav'd thence ;
But blessedly holp hither.[9]
    Mira.   O, my heart bleeds
To think o' the teen [10] that I have turn'd you to,
Which is from my remembrance ! Please you, further.
    Pros. My brother, and thy uncle, call'd Antonio, —
I pray thee, mark me ; — that a brother should
Be so perfidious ! — he whom, next thyself,
Of all the world I lov'd, and to him put
The manage of my State ; as, at that time,
Through all the signiories it was the first,[11]
And Prospero the prime Duke ; being so reputed
In dignity, and for the liberal arts
Without a parallel : those being all my study,
The government I cast upon my brother,
And to my State grew stranger, being transported
And rapt in secret studies. Thy false uncle —
Dost thou attend me ?
    Mira.   Sir, most heedfully.
    Pros. Being once perfected how to grant suits,
How to deny them ; who t' advance, and who
To trash [12] for over-topping, — new-created
The creatures that were mine, I say, or chang'd 'em,
Or else new-form'd 'em ; having both the key
Of officer and office, set all hearts i' the State
To what tune pleas'd his ear ; that [13] now he was
The ivy which had hid my princely trunk,
And suck'd the verdure out on't. Thou attend'st not.[14]
    Mira. O good sir, I do.

---

[9] *Holp* and *holpen* were continually used in the Poet's time for *helped.* The English *Psalter* abounds in instances of such use.

[10] *Teen* is an old word for *trouble, anxiety,* or *sorrow.*

[11] Botero, in his *Relations of the World,* 1630, says : "Milan claims to be the first duchy in Europe."

[12] *To trash* means to check the pace or progress of any one. *Trashes* are clogs strapped round the neck of a dog to prevent his overspeed.

[13] *That* is continually used in old poetry with the force of *so that,* or *insomuch that.*

[14] The dear old man seems to think his daughter is not attending to his tale, because his own thoughts keep wandering from it ; his mind being filled with other things, — the tempest he has got up, and the consequences of it. This absence of mind is well indicated also by the irregular and broken course of his narrative.

Pros.   I pray thee, mark me.
I thus neglecting worldly ends, all dedicated
To closeness, and the bettering of my mind
With that which, but by being so retir'd,
O'er-priz'd all popular rate,[15] in my false brother
Awak'd an evil nature ; and my trust,
Like a good parent, did beget of him
A falsehood, in its contrary as great
As my trust was ; which had indeed no limit,
A confidence sans bound.   He being thus lorded,
Not only with what my revenue yielded,[16]
But what my power might else exact, — like one
Who having, unto truth, by telling of it,[17]
Made such a sinner of his memory,
To credit his own lie, — he did believe
He was indeed the Duke ; out o' the substitution,
And executing the outward face of royalty,
With all prerogative : Hence his ambition growing, —
Dost thou hear ?
Mira.   Your tale, sir, would cure deafness.
Pros. To have no screen between this part he play'd
And him he play'd it for, he needs will be
Absolute Milan.   Me, poor man, my library
Was dukedom large enough : [18] of temporal royalties
He thinks me now incapable ; confederates
(So dry he was for sway) wi' th' King of Naples
To give him annual tribute, do him homage,
Subject his coronet to his crown, and bend
The dukedom, yet unbow'd, — alas, poor Milan ! —
To most ignoble stooping.
Mira.   O the Heavens !
Pros. Mark his condition, and th' event ; then tell me,
If this might be a brother.
Mira.   I should sin
To think but nobly of my grandmother :
Good wombs have borne bad sons.

[15] The meaning seems to be : "Which would have exceeded all popular estimate, but that it withdrew me from my public duties " ; as if he were sensible of his error in getting so "rapt in secret studies " as to leave the State a prey to violence and usurpation.

[16] Shakespeare, in a few places, has *revenue* with the first syllable long, in accordance with the vulgar pronunciation of our time.   Here the accent is on the second syllable, as it ought to be.   See vol. i. page 574, note 8.

[17] *It* here refers to *lie* in the second line below.   So that the meaning is : "Who, having made his memory such a sinner to truth by lying, that he came to believe his own lie."

[18] The meaning is, he took it into his head that my library was dukedom large enough *for* me.   *Dry*, second line below, means *thirsty* ; no uncommon use of the word even now.

Pros.   Now the condition.
This King of Naples, being an enemy
To me inveterate, hearkens my brother's suit;
Which was, that he, in lieu o' the premises,[19] —
Of homage, and I know not how much tribute, —
Should presently extirpate me and mine
Out of the dukedom; and confer fair Milan,
With all the honours, on my brother: whereon,
A treacherous army levied, one midnight
Fated to th' practice, did Antonio open
The gates of Milan; [20] and, i' the dead of darkness,
The ministers for th' purpose hurried thence
Me and thy crying self.
    Mira.   Alack, for pity!
I, not remembering how I cried on't then,
Will cry it o'er again: it is a hint,
That wrings mine eyes to't.
    Pros.   Hear a little further,
And then I'll bring thee to the present business
Which now's upon's; without the which, this story
Were most impertinent.
    Mira.   Wherefore did they not
That hour destroy us ?
    Pros.   Well demanded, wench:
My tale provokes that question. Dear, they durst not, —
So dear the love my people bore me, — nor set
A mark so bloody on the business; but
With colours fairer painted their foul ends.
In few, they hurried us aboard a bark,
Bore us some leagues to sea; where they prepar'd
A rotten carcass of a boat, not rigg'd,
Nor tackle, sail, nor mast; the very rats
Instinctively had quit it: there they hoist us,
To cry to th' sea that roar'd to us; to sigh
To th' winds, whose pity, sighing back again,
Did us but loving wrong.
    Mira.   Alack, what trouble
Was I then to you!
    Pros.   O, a cherubin
Thou wast that did preserve me! Thou didst smile,
Infused with a fortitude from Heaven,

---

[19] In *consideration* of the premises. *Lieu* was commonly used thus in the Poet's time. See vol. i. page 161, note 31.

[20] Here, instead of *practice*, the original has *purpose*, the word having probably got misprinted from *purpose* in the following clause. The change is adopted by Dyce from Collier's second folio. *Practice* means *contrivance* or *conspiracy*. *Hint*, in the next speech, is used for *cause* or *subject*. So, afterwards in this play, "Our *hint* of woe."

When I have deck'd [21] the sea with drops full salt,
Under my burden groan'd; which rais'd in me
An undergoing stomach,[22] to bear up
Against what should ensue.
   Mira.   How came we ashore?
   Pros. By Providence divine.
Some food we had, and some fresh water, that
A noble Neapolitan, Gonzalo,
Out of his charity, (who being then appointed
Master of this design,) did give us; with
Rich garments, linens, stuffs, and necessaries,
Which since have steaded much: so, of his gentleness,
Knowing I lov'd my books, he furnish'd me,
From mine own library, with volumes that
I prize above my dukedom.
   Mira.   Would I might
But ever see that man!
   Pros. [*Resuming his Robe.*]   Now I arise:
Sit still, and hear the last of our sea-sorrow.
Here in this island we arriv'd; and here
Have I, thy schoolmaster, made thee more profit [23]
Than other princes can, that have more time
For vainer hours, and tutors not so careful.
   Mira. Heavens thank you for't!   And now, I pray
           you, sir, —
For still 'tis beating in my mind, — your reason
For raising this sea-storm?
   Pros.   Know thus far forth:
By accident most strange, bountiful Fortune —
Now my dear lady — hath mine enemies
Brought to this shore; and by my prescience
I find my zenith [24] doth depend upon
A most auspicious star, whose influence
If now I court not, but omit, my fortunes
Will ever after droop.   Here cease more questions:
Thou art inclin'd to sleep; 't is a good dulness,
And give it way: — I know thou canst not choose. —
                        [MIRANDA *sleeps.*

---

[21] This word *deck'd* has given the editors a deal of trouble, as neither of its admitted senses at all suits the context.   It appears that the old Craven dialect has the word *deg*, meaning to *sprinkle*.   Mr. Dyce, therefore, notes upon the passage thus: "Here *deck'd* would seem to be a form, if it be not a corruption, of the provincialism *degg'd*, that is, *sprinkled.*

[22] An undergoing *stomach* is a firm, resolute, enduring *courage.*   The Poet often uses *stomach* thus.

[23] *Profit* is here a verb; have made thee to profit more.

[24] In astrological language *zenith* is the *highest point* in one's fortunes.

Come away, servant, come! I'm ready now:
Approach, my Ariel; come!

Enter ARIEL.

Ari. All hail, great master! grave sir, hail! I come
To answer thy best pleasure; be't to fly,
To swim, to dive into the fire, to ride
On the curl'd clouds: to thy strong bidding task
Ariel and all his quality.[25]
 Pros.   Hast thou, spirit,
Perform'd to point [26] the tempest that I bade thee?
 Ari. To every article.
I boarded the King's ship; now on the beak,
Now in the waist,[27] the deck, in every cabin,
I flam'd amazement: sometime I'd divide,
And burn in many places; on the top-mast,
The yards, and bowsprit, would I flame distinctly,[28]
Then meet, and join. Jove's lightnings, the precursors
O' the dreadful thunder-claps, more momentary [29]
And sight-outrunning were not: the fire, and cracks
Of sulphurous roaring, the most mighty Neptune
Seem'd to besiege, and make his bold waves tremble,
Yea, his dread trident shake.
 Pros.   My brave spirit!
Who was so firm, so constant, that this coil [30]
Would not infect his reason?
 Ari.   Not a soul
But felt a fever of the mad,[31] and play'd
Some tricks of desperation. All but mariners
Plung'd in the foaming brine, and quit the vessel,
Then all a-fire with me: the King's son, Ferdinand,
With hair up-staring,[32] — then like reeds, not hair, —
Was the first man that leap'd; cried, *Hell is empty,*
And all the devils are here.

---

[25] "All his *quality*" is all of his *kind*, all his *fellow-spirits*, or who are like him.

[26] Perform'd *exactly*, or in *every point;* from the French *à point.*

[27] *Beak*, the prow of the ship; *waist*, the part between the quarter-deck and forecastle.

[28] So in the account of Robert Tomson's voyage, 1555, quoted by Mr. Hunter: "This light continued aboard our ship about three hours, flying from mast to mast, and from top to top; and sometimes it would be in two or three places at once."

[29] *Momentary* in the sense of *instantaneous.*

[30] *Coil* is *stir, tumult,* or *disturbance.* See vol. i. page 569, note 4.

[31] Such a fever as madmen feel when the frantic fit is on them.

[32] *Upstaring* is *sticking out* "like quills upon the fretful porpentine." So in *The Faerie Queene*, vi. 11, 27: "With ragged weedes, and *locks upstaring* hye." See vol. i. page 496, note 22.

Pros.   Why, that's my spirit !
But was not this nigh shore ?
    Ari.   Close by, my master.
    Pros. But are they, Ariel, safe ?
    Ari.   Not a hair perish'd ;
On their sustaining garments [33] not a blemish,
But fresher than before : and, as thou bad'st me,
In troops I have dispers'd them 'bout the isle.
The King's son have I landed by himself ;
Whom I left cooling of the air with sighs
In an odd angle of the isle, and sitting,
His arms in this sad knot.[34]
    Pros.   Of the King's ship
The mariners, say, how hast thou dispos'd,
And all the rest o' the fleet ?
    Ari.   Safely in harbour
Is the King's ship ; in the deep nook, where once
Thou call'dst me up at midnight to fetch dew
From the still-vex'd Bermoothes,[35] there she's hid :
The mariners all under hatches stow'd ;
Who, with a charm join'd to their suffer'd labour,
I've left asleep : and for the rest o' the fleet,
Which I dispers'd, they all have met again,
And are upon the Mediterranean flote,[36]
Bound sadly home for Naples ;
Supposing that they saw the King's ship wreck'd,
And his great person perish.
    Pros.   Ariel, thy charge
Exactly is perform'd : but there's more work.
What is the time o' the day ?
    Ari.   Past the mid season,
At least two glasses.[37]
    Pros.   The time 'twixt six and now
Must by us both be spent most preciously.

[33] Probably the garments that *bore them up* in the water.
[34] His arms folded up as in sorrowful meditation.
[35] *Still-vex'd* is *ever-troubled.* The Poet very often uses *still* in the sense
of *ever* or *continually.* The Bermudas were supposed to be inhabited or
haunted by witches and devils, and the sea around them to be agitated with
perpetual storms. *Bermoothes* was then the common spelling of *Bermudas.*
So in Fletcher's *Women Pleased,* i. 2:

> "The devil should think of purchasing that egg-shell,
>   To victual such a witch for the *Burmoothes.*"

[36] *Flote* is said to be a substantive, meaning *flood, wave,* or *sea.* This
passage shows that the scene of the play is *not* laid in the Bermudas, as
there has not been time for the rest of the fleet to sail so far. And Ariel's
trip to fetch the dew mentioned above was a much greater feat than going
from one part of the Bermoothes to another.
[37] *Two glasses* is *two runnings* of the hour-glass. The original prints these
words, " At least two glasses," as part of Prospero's next speech.

Ari. Is there more toil? Since thou dost give me pains,
Let me remember thee what thou hast promis'd,
Which is not yet perform'd me.
    Pros.   How now! moody?
What is't thou canst demand?
    Ari.   My liberty.
    Pros. Before the time be out? no more!
    Ari.   I pr'ythee,
Remember I have done thee worthy service;
Told thee no lies, made no mistakings, serv'd
Without or grudge or grumblings: Thou didst promise
To bate me a full year.
    Pros.   Dost thou forget
From what a torment I did free thee?
    Ari.   No.
    Pros. Thou dost; and think'st it much to tread the ooze
Of the salt deep;
To run upon the sharp wind of the north;
To do me business in the veins o' the earth
When it is bak'd with frost.
    Ari.   I do not, sir.
    Pros. Thou liest, malignant thing! Hast thou forgot
The foul witch Sycorax, who with age and envy
Was grown into a hoop? hast thou forgot her?
    Ari. No, sir.
    Pros.   Thou hast: Where was she born?
        speak; tell me.
    Ari. Sir, in Argier.[88]
    Pros.   O, was she so? I must
Once in a month recount what thou hast been,
Which thou forgett'st. This damn'd witch Sycorax,
For mischiefs manifold, and sorceries terrible
To enter human hearing, from Argier,
Thou know'st, was banish'd: for one thing she did,
They would not take her life. Is not this true?
    Ari. Ay, sir.
    Pros. This blue-ey'd [89] hag was hither brought,
And here was left by th' sailors. Thou, my slave,
As thou report'st thyself, wast then her servant;
And, for thou wast a spirit too delicate
To act her earthy and abhorr'd commands,

---

[88] *Argier* is the old English name of *Algiers.*
[89] What are now called *blue* eyes were called *gray* in the Poet's time; and *blue-ey'd* was used in a very different sense from what it now bears. Blue eyes were considered eminently beautiful; but here the term signifies great ugliness; that is, *blueness about the eyes.* So in *As you Like It,* iii. 2: " A *blue eye,* and a sunken." See vol. i. page 64, note 88; also page 190, note 21.

Refusing her grand hests, she did confine thee,
By help of her more potent ministers,
And in her most unmitigable rage,
Into a cloven pine; [40] within which rift
Imprison'd thou didst painfully remain
A dozen years; within which space she died,
And left thee there; where thou didst vent thy groans
As fast as mill-wheels strike. Then was this island —
Save for the son that she did litter here,
A freckled whelp, hag-born — not honour'd with
A human shape.

   Ari.   Yes, Caliban her son.

   Pros. Dull thing, I say so; he, that Caliban,
Whom now I keep in service. Thou best know'st
What torment I did find thee in: thy groans
Did make wolves howl, and penetrate the breasts
Of ever-angry bears. It was a torment
To lay upon the damn'd, which Sycorax
Could not again undo: it was mine art,
When I arriv'd and heard thee, that made gape
The pine, and let thee out.

   Ari.   I thank thee, master.

   Pros. If thou more murmur'st, I will rend an oak,
And peg thee in his knotty entrails, till
Thou'st howl'd away twelve Winters.

   Ari.   Pardon, master:
I will be correspondent to command,
And do my spriting gently.

   Pros.   Do so; and after two days
I will discharge thee.

   Ari.   That 's my noble master!
What shall I do? say what; what shall I do?

   Pros. Go make thyself like to a nymph o' the sea:
Be subject to no sight but mine; invisible
To every eyeball else. Go take this shape,
And hither come in't: hence, with diligence —!

                        [*Exit* ARIEL.
Awake, dear heart, awake! thou hast slept well;
Awake!

   Mira. [*Waking.*] The strangeness of your story put
Heaviness in me.

   Pros.   Shake it off: come on;
We'll visit Caliban my slave, who never
Yields us kind answer.

   [40] In such cases the Poet uses *into* or *in* indifferently, as suits his verse. —
Hests, fourth line above, is *commands, behests.* See vol. i. page 277, note 7.

   Mira.   'Tis a villain, sir,
I do not love to look on.
   Pros.   But, as 'tis,
We cannot miss him : [41] he does make our fire,
Fetch in our wood, and serves in offices
That profit us. — What ho ! slave ! Caliban !
Thou earth, thou ! speak.
   Cal. [*Within.*] There's wood enough within.
   Pros. Come forth, I say ! there's other business for
       thee :
Come forth, thou tortoise ! when ? [42] —

Re-enter ARIEL, *like a Water-nymph.*

Fine apparition ! My quaint Ariel, [43]
Hark in thine ear.
   Ari.   My lord, it shall be done.   [*Exit.*
   Pros. Thou poisonous slave, come forth !

Enter CALIBAN.

   Cal. As wicked dew as e'er my mother brush'd
With raven's feather from unwholesome fen
Drop on you both ! a southwest blow on ye,
And blister you all o'er !
   Pros. For this, be sure, to-night thou shalt have
       cramps,
Side-stitches that shall pen thy breath up ; urchins [44]
Shall, for that vast [45] of night that they may work,
All exercise on thee : thou shalt be pinch'd
As thick as honeycomb, each pinch more stinging
Than bees that made 'em.
   Cal.   I must eat my dinner.
This island's mine, by Sycorax my mother,
Which thou tak'st from me. When thou cam'st here
       first,
Thou strok'dst me, and mad'st much of me ; would'st
       give me

---

[41] We cannot *do without* him. The phrase is said to be common still in some parts of England.

[42] *When* was sometimes used as an exclamation of impatience. See vol. i. page 449, note 2.

[43] *Quaint*, as here used, is *ingenious, artful, cunning.* See vol. i. page 546, note 3.

[44] *Urchins* were fairies of a particular class. Hedgehogs were also called *urchins;* and it is probable that the sprites were so named, because they were of a mischievous kind, the *urchin* being anciently deemed a very noxious animal.

[45] So in *Hamlet*, i. 2, "in the dead *vast* and middle of the night"; meaning the silent void or vacancy of night, when spirits were anciently supposed to walk abroad on errands of love or sport or mischief.

Water with berries in't; and teach me how
To name the bigger light, and how the less,
That burn by day and night: and then I lov'd thee,
And show'd thee all the qualities o' the isle,
The fresh springs, brine pits, barren place, and fertile:
Cursed be I that did so! All the charms
Of Sycorax, toads, beetles, bats, light on you!
For I am all the subjects that you have,
Which first was mine own king: and here you sty me
In this hard rock, whiles you do keep from me
The rest o' the island.
  Pros.   Thou most lying slave,
Whom stripes may move, not kindness, I have us'd thee,
Filth as thou art, with human care; and lodg'd thee
In mine own cell, till thou didst seek to violate
The honour of my child.
  Cal. O ho, O ho! — would 't had been done!
Thou didst prevent me.
  Pros.   Abhorred slave,
Which any print of goodness will not take,
Being capable of all ill! I pitied thee,
Took pains to make thee speak, taught thee each hour
One thing or other: when thou didst not, savage,
Know thine own meaning, but would'st gabble like
A thing most brutish, I endow'd thy purposes
With words that made them known. But thy vile race,
Though thou didst learn, had that in't which good natures
Could not abide to be with; therefore wast thou
Confin'd into this rock, who hadst deserv'd
More than a prison.
  Cal. You taught me language; and my profit on't
Is, I know how to curse. The red plague rid you [46]
For learning me your language!
  Pros.-   Hag-seed, hence!
Fetch us in fuel; and be quick, thou'rt best,
To answer other business. Shrugg'st thou, malice?
If thou neglect'st, or dost unwillingly
What I command, I'll rack thee with old cramps, [47]
Fill all thy bones with aches, [48] make thee roar,
That beasts shall tremble at thy din.
  Cal.   No, pray thee! —

---

[46] *Rid* here means *destroy.* So in *King Richard II.*, v. 4. "I am the King's friend, and will *rid* his foe."

[47] *Old* was often used as an augmentative, meaning *great, abundant.* See vol. i. page 163, note 2.

[48] *Ache* was formerly pronounced like the letter *H.* The plural *aches* was therefore a word of two syllables, as the verse requires it to be here. We

[*Aside.*] I must obey: his art is of such power,
It would control my dam's god, Setebos,[49]
And make a vassal of him.
    Pros.   So, slave; hence!.
                       [*Exit* CALIBAN.

Re-enter ARIEL *invisible, playing and singing ;*

FERDINAND *following.*

ARIEL'S *Song.*

Come unto these yellow sands,
   And then take hands :
Curtsied when you have, and kiss'd
   The wild waves whist,[50]
Foot it featly here and there ;
And, sweet sprites, the burden bear.
   Hark, hark !
Burden.   [*Dispersedly, within.*] Bow, wow.
       The watch-dogs bark :
Burden.   [*Dispersedly, within.*] Bow, wow.
    Hark, hark ! I hear
    The strain of strutting chanticleer
    Cry, Cock-a-diddle-doo.

Ferd. Where should this music be? i' the air, or th'
    earth ?
It sounds no more : — and, sure, it waits upon
Some god o' the island. Sitting on a bank,
Weeping again the King my father's wreck,
This music crept by me upon the waters,
Allaying both their fury and my passion

have many instances of such pronunciation in the old writers. Thus in *Antony and Cleopatra*, iv. 7: "I had a wound here that was like a T, but now 'tis made an H." It is said that Kemble the actor undertook to revive the old pronunciation of *aches* on the stage; but the audience would not stand it, and hissed him out of it. However correct literally, the attempt, it must be confessed, savoured more of pedantry than of good judgment.

[49] *Setebos* was the name of an American god, or rather devil, worshipped by the Patagonians. In Eden's *History of Travaile*, 1577, is an account of Magellan's voyage to the South Pole, containing a description of this god and his worshippers; wherein the author says: "When they felt the shackles fast about their legs, they began to doubt; but the captain did put them in comfort and bade them stand still. In fine, when they saw how they were deceived, they roared like bulls, and cryed upon their *great devil Setebos*, to help them."

[50] So printed in the original; meaning, apparently, "Kiss'd the wild waves *into stillness* or *peace.*" In modern editions generally "The wild waves whist" is made parenthetical, so as to mean "The wild waves *being* whist." This, it seems to me, without bettering the sense, expunges a delicate touch of poetry that is well worth keeping.

With its sweet air : thence I have follow'd it,
Or it hath drawn me rather : — but 'tis gone.
No, it begins again.

ARIEL *sings.*

Full fathom five thy father lies ;
 Of his bones are coral made ;
Those are pearls that were his eyes :
 Nothing of him that doth fade,
But doth suffer a sea-change
Into something rich and strange.
Sea-nymphs hourly ring his knell :
Burden. [*Within.*]   Ding-dong.
 Hark ! now I hear them, — ding-dong, bell.

Ferd. The ditty does remember my drown'd father :—
This is no mortal business, nor no sound
That the earth owes : [51] — I hear it now above me.
 Pros. The fringed curtains of thine eye advance,
And say what thou seest yond.
 Mira.   What is't ? a spirit ?
Lord, how it looks about ! Believe me, sir,
It carries a brave form : — but 'tis a spirit.
 Pros. No, wench ; [52] it eats and sleeps, and hath such
  senses
As we have, such. This gallant which thou seest
Was in the wreck ; and, but [53] he's something stain'd
With grief, that's beauty's canker, thou might'st call him
A goodly person. He· hath lost his fellows,
And strays about to find 'em.
 Mira.   I might call him
A thing divine ; for nothing natural
I ever saw so noble.
 Pros. [*Aside.*] It goes on, I see,
As my soul prompts it. — Spirit, fine spirit ! I'll free thee
Within two days for this.
 Ferd.   Most sure, the goddess
On whom these airs attend ! — Vouchsafe my prayer
May know if you remain upon this island ;
And that you will some good instruction give
How I may bear me here : My prime request,

---

[51] To *owe* was to *possess* or *own*, in ancient language.
[52] *Wench* was often used thus as a term of playful familiarity, without implying anything of reproach or contempt.
[53] This is the exceptive *but*, as it is called ; formed from *be out*, and meaning *except that*. So, once before in this scene : "The bettering of my mind with that which, *but* by being so retir'd, o'erpriz'd all popular rate."

2

Which I do last pronounce, is, — O you wonder! —
If you be maid [54] or no?
   Mira.   No wonder, sir;
But certainly a maid.
   Ferd.   My language! Heavens! —
I am the best of them that speak this speech,
Were I but where 'tis spoken.
   Pros.   How! the best!
What wert thou, if the King of Naples heard thee?
   Ferd. A single thing,[55] as I am now, that wonders
To hear thee speak of Naples. He does hear me;
And that he does I weep: myself am Naples;
Who with mine eyes, ne'er since at ebb, beheld
The King my father wreck'd.
   Mira.   Alack, for mercy!
   Ferd. Yes, faith, and all his lords; the Duke of Milan
And his brave son being twain.[56]
   Pros. [*Aside.*]   The Duke of Milan
And his more braver daughter could control thee,[57]
If now 'twere fit to do't. — At the first sight
They have chang'd eyes. — Delicate Ariel,
I'll set thee free for this! — A word, good sir:
I fear you've done yourself some wrong:[58] a word.
   Mira. [*Aside.*] Why speaks my father so ungently?
      This
Is the third man that e'er I saw; the first
That e'er I sigh'd for: Pity move my father
To be inclin'd my way!
   Fer.   O, if a virgin,
And your affection not gone forth, I'll make you
The Queen of Naples.
   Pros.   Soft, sir! one word more. —
[*Aside.*] They're both in either's powers: but this swift
      business
I must uneasy make, lest too light winning

[54] Ferdinand has already spoken of Miranda as a goddess: he now asks, if she be a mortal; not a celestial being, but a maiden. Of course her answer is to be taken in the same sense as his question. The name *Miranda* literally signifies *wonderful.*

[55] *A weak, feeble* thing. The Poet elsewhere uses *single* in this sense; as in *Macbeth:* "Shakes so my *single* state of man."

[56] This young man, the son of Antonio, nowhere appears in the play, nor is there any other mention of him. Perhaps he was in one of the other ships, and Ferdinand supposes him lost in the general wreck of the fleet.

[57] To *control* was formerly used in the sense of to *refute;* from the French *contre-roller,* to exhibit a *contrary account.* Prospero means that he could refute what Ferdinand has just said about the Duke of Milan. *Braver* is probably used in the sense of *finer;* a common meaning of the word.

[58] Done wrong to your character, in claiming to be King of Naples.

Make the prize light. — One word more; I charge thee
That thou attend me : Thou dost here usurp
The name thou ow'st not; and hast put thyself
Upon this island as a spy, to win it
From me, the lord on't.
    Ferd.   No, as I'm a man.
    Mira. There's nothing ill can dwell in such a temple :
If the ill spirit have so fair a house,
Good things will strive to dwell with't.
    Pros. [*To* FERD.]   Follow me. —
Speak not you for him; he's a traitor. — Come;
I'll manacle thy neck and feet together :
Sea-water shalt thou drink; thy food shall be
The fresh-brook muscles, wither'd roots, and husks
Wherein the acorn cradled : Follow.
    Ferd.   No;
I will resist such entertainment, till
Mine enemy has more power.
            [*He draws, and is charmed from moving.*
    Mira.   O dear father,
Make not too rash a trial of him, for
He's gentle, and not fearful.[59]
    Pros.   What, I say,
My fool my tutor! — Put thy sword up, traitor;
Who mak'st a show, but dar'st not strike, thy conscience
Is so possess'd with guilt : come from thy ward;[60]
For I can here disarm thee with this stick,
And make thy weapon drop.
    Mira.   Beseech you, father! —
    Pros. Hence! hang not on my garments.
    Mira.   Sir, have pity;
I'll be his surety.
    Pros.   Silence! one word more
Shall make me chide thee, if not hate thee. What,
An advocate for an impostor! hush!
Thou think'st there are no more such shapes as he,
Having seen but him and Caliban : foolish wench!
To th' most of men this is a Caliban,
And they to him are angels.
    Mira.   My affections
Are, then, most humble : I have no ambition
To see a goodlier man.

[59] This clearly means that Ferdinand is brave and high-spirited, so that, if pressed too hard, he will rather die than succumb. It is a good old notion that bravery and gentleness naturally go together.
[60] *Ward* is *posture* or *attitude of defence.* See vol. i. page 288, note 20.

Pros. [*To* FERD.]　　Come on; obey:
Thy nerves are in their infancy again,
And have no vigour in them.
　Ferd.　　　　　　　　So they are:
My spirits, as in a dream, are all bound up.
My father's loss, the weakness which I feel,
The wreck of all my friends, and this man's threats
To whom I am subdu'd, are light to me,
Might I but through my prison once a day
Behold this maid : all corners else o' the earth
Let liberty make use of; space enough
Have I in such a prison.
　Pros. [*Aside.*] It works.—[*To* FERD.] Come on.—
Thou hast done well, fine Ariel!—Follow me.—
[*To* ARIEL.]　Hark, what thou else shalt do me.
　Mira.　　　　　　　　Be of comfort ;[61]
My father's of a better nature, sir,
Than he appears by speech : this is unwonted
Which now came from him.
　Pros. [*To* ARIEL.]　　Thou shalt be as free
As mountain winds : but then exactly do
All points of my command.
　Ari.　　　　　　　To th' syllable.
　Pros. Come, follow.— Speak not for him.　　[*Exeunt.*

ACT II.　SCENE I.　*Another part of the Island.*

Enter ALONSO, SEBASTIAN, ANTONIO, GONZALO, ADRIAN,
FRANCISCO, *and others.*

　Gon. Beseech you, sir, be merry : you have cause —
So have we all — of joy ; for our escape
Is much beyond our loss.　Our hint of woe
Is common ; every day some sailor's wife,
The master of some merchant,[1] and the merchant,
Have just our theme of woe: but for the miracle —
I mean our preservation — few in millions
Can speak like us : then wisely, good sir, weigh
Our sorrow with our comfort.
　Alon.　　　　　　　Pr'ythee, peace.

---

[61] *Be of comfort* is old language for *be comforted.*　See vol. i. page 226,
note 7.
　[1] It was usual to call a *merchant-vessel* a *merchant,* as we now say a *mer-
chant-man.*

Seb. He receives comfort like cold porridge.

Ant. The visitor[2] will not give him o'er so.

Seb. Look, he's winding up the watch of his wit; by-and-by it will strike.

Gon. Sir, —

Seb. One : — tell.

Gon. — When every grief is entertain'd that's offer'd,
Comes to the entertainer —

Seb.   A dollar.

Gon. Dolour comes to him, indeed : you have spoken truer than you purpos'd.

Seb. You have taken it wiselier than I meant you should.

Gon. Therefore, my lord, —

Ant. Fie, what a spendthrift is he of his tongue!

Alon. I pr'ythee, spare me.

Gon. Well, I have done : but yet —

Seb. He will be talking.

Ant. Which of he or Adrian, for a good wager, first begins to crow ?

Seb. The old cock.

Ant. The cockerel.

Seb. Done! The wager?

Ant. A laughter.

Seb. A match!

Adr. Though this island seem to be desert, —

Seb. Ha, ha, ha! — So, you're paid.[3]

Adr. — uninhabitable, and almost inaccessible, —

Seb. Yet —

Adr. — yet —

Ant. He could not miss't.

Adr. — it must needs be of subtle, tender, and delicate temperance.[4]

Ant. Temperance was a delicate wench.

Seb. Ay, and a subtle; as he most learnedly delivered.

Adr. The air breathes upon us here most sweetly.

Seb. As if it had lungs, and rotten ones.

Ant. Or as 'twere perfum'd by a fen.

---

[2] He calls Gonzalo the *visitor*, in allusion to the office of one who visits the sick to give advice and consolation. — *Tell*, third speech below, is *count*, or *keep tally*; referring to "the watch of his wit," which he was said to be "winding up," and which now begins to strike.

[3] A laugh having been agreed upon as the wager, and Sebastian having lost, he now pays with a laugh. The original wrongly assigns the words, "So, you're paid," to Antonio.

[4] By *temperance* Adrian means *temperature*, and Antonio plays upon the word; alluding, perhaps, to the Puritan custom of bestowing the names of the cardinal virtues upon their children.

Gon. Here is every thing advantageous to life.

Ant. True; save means to live.

Seb. Of that there's none, or little.

Gon. How lush [5] and lusty the grass looks! how green!

Ant. The ground, indeed, is tawny.

Seb. With an eye of green in 't. [6]

Ant. He misses not much.

Seb. No; he doth but mistake the truth totally.

Gon. But the rarity of it is, — which is indeed almost beyond credit, —

Seb. As many vouch'd rarities are.

Gon. — that our garments, being, as they were, drenched in the sea, hold, notwithstanding, their freshness and gloss; being rather new-dyed than stain'd with salt water.

Ant. If but one of his pockets could speak, would it not say he lies?

Seb. Ay, or very falsely pocket up his report.

Gon. Methinks our garments are now as fresh as when we put them on first in Afric, at the marriage of the King's fair daughter Claribel to the King of Tunis.

Seb. 'Twas a sweet marriage, and we prosper well in our return.

Adr. Tunis was never grac'd before with such a paragon to their Queen. [7]

Gon. Not since widow Dido's time.

Ant. Widow? a pox o' that! How came that widow in? Widow Dido!

Seb. What if he had said widower Æneas too? Good Lord, how you take it!

Adr. Widow Dido, said you? you make me study of that: she was of Carthage, not of Tunis.

Gon. This Tunis, sir, was Carthage.

Adr. Carthage!

Gon. I assure you, Carthage.

Ant. His word is more than the miraculous harp. [8]

---

[5] *Lush* is *juicy, succulent*, — luxuriant.

[6] A *tint* or *shade* of green. So in Sandy's *Travels:* "Cloth of silver, tissued with an *eye* of green"; and Bayle says: "Red with an *eye* of blue makes a purple."

[7] *To* was continually used in such cases where we should use *for*. So in the Marriage Office of the Episcopal Church: "Wilt thou have this woman *to* thy wedded wife?" Also, in *St. Mark*, xii. 23: "The seven had her *to* wife."

[8] Amphion, King of Thebes, was a prodigious musician: god Mercury gave him a lyre, with which he charmed the stones into their places, and thus built the walls of the city: as Wordsworth puts it, "The gift to King

Seb. He hath rais'd the wall, and houses too.

Ant. What impossible matter will he make easy next?

Seb. I think he will carry this island home in his pocket, and give it his son for an apple.

Ant. And, sowing the kernels of it in the sea, bring forth more islands.

Alon. Ah![9]

Ant. Why, in good time.

Gon. Sir, we were talking that our garments seem now as fresh as when we were at Tunis at the marriage of your daughter, who is now Queen.

Ant. And the rarest that e'er came there.

Seb. Bate, I beseech you, widow Dido.

Ant. O, widow Dido; ay, widow Dido.

Gon. Is not, sir, my doublet as fresh as the first day I wore it? I mean, in a sort.

Ant. That sort was well fish'd for.[10]

Gon. When I wore it at your daughter's marriage?

Alon. You cram these words into mine ears against
The stomach of my sense. Would I had never
Married my daughter there! for, coming thence,
My son is lost; and, in my rate, she too,
Who is so far from Italy remov'd,
I ne'er again shall see her. O thou mine heir
Of Naples and of Milan, what strange fish
Hath made his meal on thee?

Fran.   Sir, he may live:
I saw him beat the surges under him,
And ride upon their backs; he trod the water,
Whose enmity he flung aside, and breasted
The surge most swoln that met him; his bold head
'Bove the contentious waves he kept, and oar'd
Himself with his good arms in lusty stroke
To th' shore, that o'er his wave-worn basis bow'd,
As stooping to relieve him. I not doubt
He came alive to land.

Alon.   No, no; he's gone.

Seb. Sir, you may thank yourself for this great loss,
That would not bless our Europe with your daughter,

Amphion, that walled a city with its melody." Tunis is in fact supposed
to be on or near the site of ancient Carthage.

[9] The original assigns to Gonzalo this sigh or groan expressed by *Ah!*
The correction is Mr. Staunton's, who says, "this exclamation belongs to
Alonso, who is awaking from his trance of grief."

[10] A quibbling allusion, probably, to one of the meanings of *sort*, which
was *lot* or *portion*, from the Latin *sors*. See vol. i. page 107, note 15.

But rather lose her to an African ;
Where she at least is banish'd from your eye,
Who hath cause to wet the grief on't.[11]
 Alon.   Pr'ythee, peace.
 Seb. You were kneel'd to, and impórtun'd otherwise,
By all of us ; and the fair soul herself
Weigh'd, between loathness and obedience, at
Which end the beam should bow [12] We've lost your
   son,
I fear, for ever : Milan and Naples have
More widows in them of this business' making
Than we bring men to comfort them : the fault's
Your own.
 Alon. So is the dear'st o' the loss.
 Gon.   My Lord Sebastian,
The truth you speak doth lack some gentleness,
And time to speak it in : you rub the sore,
When you should bring the plaster.
 Seb.   Very well.
 Ant. And most chirurgeonly.[13]
 Gon. It is foul weather in us all, good sir,
When you are cloudy.
 Seb.   Foul weather !
 Ant.   Very foul.
 Gon. Had I plantation [14] of this isle, my lord, —
 Ant. He'd sow't with nettle-seed.
 Seb.   Or docks, or mallows.
 Gon. — And were the King on't, what would I do ?
 Seb. 'Scape being drunk for want of wine.
 Gon. I' the commonwealth I would by contraries
Execute all things : for no kind of traffic
Would I admit ; no name of magistrate ;
Letters should not be known ; riches, poverty,
And use of service, none ; contract, succession,
Bourn, bound of land, tilth, vineyard, none ;
No use of metal, corn, or wine, or oil ;
No occupation ; all men idle, all,

---

[11] *Who* and *which* were used indifferently both of persons and things.
Here *who* refers to *eye.*

[12] Which way the balance should turn or incline. The original reads "at
which end *o' the* beam should bow"; which is clearly wrong somewhere.
Modern editions generally change *should* to *she'd.* I think it decidedly better
to retain *should,* and change "end *o' the* beam" to "end *the* beam," thus
making *beam* the subject of *should bow.*

[13] *Chirurgeon* is the old word, which has got transformed into *surgeon.*

[14] In Shakespeare's time a *plantation* meant a *colony,* and was so used of
the American colonies. Here *plantation* is a "verbal noun," and means *the
colonizing.*

And women too, but innocent and pure;
No sovereignty : —
    Seb.   Yet he would be king on't.
    Ant. The latter end of his commonwealth forgets the
beginning.
    Gon. — All things in common Nature should produce
Without sweat or endeavour : treason, felony,
Sword, pike, knife, gun, or need of any engine,[15]
Would I not have ; but Nature should bring forth,
Of its own kind, all foison,[16] all abundance,
To feed my innocent people.
    Seb. No marrying 'mong his subjects?
    Ant. None, man ; all idle, —[trulls] and knaves.
    Gon. I would with such perfection govern, sir,
T' excel the golden age.[17]
    Seb.   God save his Majesty!
    Ant. Long live Gonzalo!
    Gon.   And, — do you mark me, sir? —
    Alon. Pr'ythee, no more : thou dost talk nothing to me.
    Gon. I do well believe your Highness ; and did it to
minister occasion to these gentlemen, who are of such
sensible and nimble lungs, that they always use to laugh
at nothing.
    Ant. 'Twas you we laugh'd at.
    Gon. Who in this kind of merry fooling am nothing
to you :[18] so you may continue, and laugh at nothing still.

---

[15] An *engine* was a term applied to any kind of *machine* in Shakespeare's age.

[16] *Foison* is only another word for *plenty* or *abundance* of provision, but chiefly of the fruits of the earth. Here, instead of "*its* own kind," the original has "*it* own kind," *it* being used as the possessive. In his earlier plays the Poet uses *his* almost constantly instead of *its*, the latter not being then an accepted word ; in his later he seems to hesitate between *his, it,* and *its.* Twice before in this play the original has *its*, but printed with an apostrophe, *it's :* "A falsehood in *it's* contrary as great" ; and "allaying both their fury and my passion with *it's* sweet air." See vol. i. page 488, note 3.

[17] In Montaigne's Essay *Of the Cannibals*, translated by Florio in 1603, is the following: "Me seemeth that what in those nations we see by experience, doth not only exceed all the pictures wherewith licentious poesy hath proudly embellished the golden age, and all her quaint inventions to feign a happy condition of man, but also the conception and desire of philosophy. — It is a nation, would I answer Plato, that hath no kind of traffic, no knowledge of letters, no intelligence of numbers, no name of magistrate, nor of politic superiority ; no use of service, of riches, or of poverty ; no contracts, no successions, no dividences ; no occupation, but idle ; no respect of kindred, but common ; no apparel, but natural ; no manuring of lands ; no use of wine, corn, or metal. The very words that import lying, falsehood, treason, dissimulation, covetousness, envy, detraction, and pardon, were never heard amongst them."

[18] Nothing *in comparison with* you. The Poet often uses *to* in this way. See vol. i. page 568, note 8.

Ant. What a blow was there given!

Seb. An it had not fallen flat-long.

Gon. You are gentlemen of brave mettle : you would lift the Moon out of her sphere, if she would[19] continue in it five weeks without changing.

Enter ARIEL, *invisible, playing solemn Music.*

Seb. We would so, and then go a-bat-fowling.[20]

Ant. Nay, good my lord, be not angry.

Gon. No, I warrant you ; I will not adventure my discretion so weakly. Will you laugh me asleep, for I am very heavy?

Ant. Go sleep, and hear us.

[*All sleep but* ALON. SEB. *and* ANT.

Alon. What, all so soon asleep! I wish mine eyes
Would, with themselves, shut up my thoughts : I find
They are inclin'd to do so.

Seb.   Please you, sir,
Do not omit the heavy offer of it :
It seldom visits sorrow ; when it doth,
It is a comforter.

Ant.   We two, my lord,
Will guard your person while you take your rest,
And watch your safety.

Alon.   Thank you. — Wondrous heavy.
[ALONSO *sleeps. Exit* ARIEL.

Seb. What a strange drowsiness possesses them !

Ant. It is the quality o' the climate.

Seb.   Why
Doth it not, then, our eyelids sink? I find not
Myself dispos'd to sleep.

Ant.   Nor I ; my spirits are nimble.
They fell together all, as by consent ;
They dropp'd, as by a thunder-stroke. What might,
Worthy Sebastian, O, what might![21] — No more : —
And yet methinks I see it in thy face,
What thou should'st be : th' occasion speaks thee ; and

---

[19] Our present idiom requires *should* instead of *would*. In Shakespeare's time, the auxiliaries *could, should,* and *would* were used *indifferently,* as were also *shall* and *will,* and some others. See vol. i. page 33, note 18, and page 586, note 7.

[20] *Bat-fowling* was a term used of catching birds in the night. This was done in various ways, one of which was, to rouse them from their nests, and surprise them with a sudden blaze of light, thus disabling them for flight.

[21] "What might *you* be," is probably the meaning here. In the second line below, *should'st* for *would'st ;* another instance of the undifferentiated use remarked in note 19.

My strong imagination sees a crown
Dropping upon thy head.
    Seb.   What, art thou waking?
    Ant. Do you not hear me speak?
    Seb.   I do; and surely
It is a sleepy language, and thou speak'st
Out of thy sleep.   What is it thou didst say?
This is a strange repose, to be asleep
With eyes wide open; standing, speaking, moving,
And yet so fast asleep.
    Ant.   Noble Sebastian,
Thou lett'st thy fortune sleep — die rather; wink'st
Whiles thou art waking.
    Seb.   Thou dost snore distinctly;
There's meaning in thy snores.
    Ant. I am more serious than my custom: you
Must be so too, if heed me; which to do
Trebles thee o'er.[22]
    Seb.   Well, I am standing water.
    Ant. I'll teach you how to flow.
    Seb.   Do so: to ebb
Hereditary sloth instructs me.
    Ant.   O,
If you but knew how you the purpose cherish
Whiles thus you mock it! how, in stripping it,
You more invest it![23]   Ebbing men, indeed,
Most often do so near the bottom run
By their own fear or sloth.
    Ant.   Pr'ythee, say on:
The setting of thine eye and cheek proclaim
A matter from thee; and a birth indeed
Which throes thee much to yield.
    Ant.   Thus, sir:
Although this lord of weak remembrance — this,
Who shall be of as little memory[24]
When he is earth'd — hath here almost persuaded
(For he's a spirit of persuasion, — only
Professes to persuade) the King his son's alive,
'Tis as impossible that he's undrown'd
As he that sleeps here swims.

[22] Makes thee three times what thou art now.

[23] Sebastian shows that he both takes and welcomes Antonio's suggestion, by his making it a theme of jest; and the more he thus denudes the hint of obscurity by playing with it, the more he clothes it with his own approval.

[24] Shall be as little remembered, or as quickly forgotten, as he is apt to forget. *Weak remembrance* means *feeble memory.* Francisco is the lord referred to.

Seb. I have no hope
That he's undrown'd.
Ant. O, out of that no hope
What great hope have you! no hope, that way, is
Another way so high a hope, that even
Ambition cannot pierce a wink beyond,
But doubts discovery there.[25] Will you grant with me
That Ferdinand is drown'd?
Seb. He's gone.
Ant. Then, tell me,
Who's the next heir of Naples?
Seb. Claribel.
Ant. She that is Queen of Tunis; she that dwells
Ten leagues beyond man's life;[26] she that from Naples
Can have no note, unless the Sun were post,
(The Man-i'-the-moon's too slow,) till new-born chins
Be rough and razorable; she from whom
We all were sea-swallow'd, though some cast again;
And, by that destiny,[27] to perform an act
Whereof what's past is prologue; what to come,
In yours and my discharge.
Seb. What stuff is this!—How say you?
'Tis true, my brother's daughter's Queen of Tunis;
So is she heir of Naples; 'twixt which regions
There is some space.
Ant. A space whose every cubit
Seems to cry out, *How shall that Claribel*
Measure us back to Naples?[28] *Keep in Tunis,*
And let Sebastian wake!— Say, this were death
That now hath seiz'd them; why, they were no worse
Than now they are. There be that can rule Naples
As well as he that sleeps; lords that can prate
As amply and unnecessarily
As this Gonzalo: I myself could make

[25] What is the meaning of *wink* and of *doubts* here? I have never met with any explanation of the passage: perhaps it is thought too clear to need explaining, but I cannot see it so. As nearly as I can find it, *wink* means the same as *jot;* cannot pierce so much beyond as may be measured by a wink of the eye: while "*doubts* discovery there" seems equivalent to "holds that there is nothing further to be discovered or desired."

[26] Beyond a lifetime of travelling. Of course this passage is a piece of intentional hyperbole; and Sebastian shows that he takes it so, by exclaiming, "What *stuff* is this!"

[27] The sense appears to be, "And, by their being cast ashore again, were destined to perform an act," &c. — "She from whom" means "she *coming* from whom"; unless *from* be a misprint for *for.*

[28] Hanmer printed, "How *shalt thou,* Claribel, measure *it* back to Naples?" which I am inclined to think the right reading, except, perhaps, the changing of *us* into *it.*

A chough of as deep chat.[29] O, that you bore
The mind that I do! what a sleep were this
For your advancement! Do you understand me?
   Seb. Methinks I do.
   Ant.   And how does your content
Tender your own good fortune?
   Seb.   I remember
You did supplant your brother Prospero.
   Ant.   True;
And look how well my garments sit upon me;
Much feater than before:[30] my brother's servants
Were then my fellows; now they are my men.
   Seb. But, for your conscience —
   Ant. Ay, sir; and where lies that? if 'twere a kibe,[31]
'Twould put me to my slipper: but I feel not
This deity in my bosom: twenty consciences,
That stand 'twixt me and Milan, candied be they,[32]
And melt, ere they molest! Here lies your brother,
No better than the earth he lies upon,
If he were that which now he's like, that's dead;
Whom I, with this obedient steel, three inches of it,
Can lay to bed for ever; whiles you, doing thus,
To the perpetual wink for aye might put
This ancient morsel, this Sir Prudence, who
Should not upbraid our course. For all the rest,
They'll take suggestion,[33] as a cat laps milk;
They'll tell the clock to any business that
We say befits the hour.
   Seb.   Thy case, dear friend,
Shall be my precedent; as thou gott'st Milan,
I'll come by Naples. Draw thy sword: one stroke
Shall free thee from the tribute which thou pay'st;
And I the King shall love thee.
   Ant.   Draw together;
And when I rear my hand, do you the like,
To fall it on Gonzalo.
   Seb.   O, but one word.
                              [*They converse apart.*

---

   [29] Could *produce, breed,* or *train* a parrot to talk as well. A *chough* is a
bird of the jackdaw kind.
   [30] *Feater* is *more trimly* or *more finely.*
   [31] The Poet has *kibe* several times for the well-known heel-sore, an
ulcerated chilblain. See vol. i. page 619, note 16.
   [32] *Candied,* here, is *congealed,* or *crystallized.* So in *Timon of Athens,*
iv. 3: "Will the cold brook, *candied with ice,* caudle thy morning taste?"
   [33] *Suggest* and its derivatives were often used in the sense of to *tempt.*
Thus Shakespeare has such phrases as "tender youth is soon *suggested,*"
and "what serpent hath *suggested* thee." The meaning of the text is,

Music.   Re-enter ARIEL, *invisible.*

Ari. My master through his art foresees the danger
That you, his friend, are in ; and sends me forth —
For else his project dies — to keep thee living.
                        [*Sings in* GONZALO'S *ear.*

> *While you here do snoring lie,*
> *Open-ey'd conspiracy*
>   *His time doth take.*
> *If of life you keep a care,*
> *Shake off slumber, and beware :*
>   *Awake ! awake !*

Ant. Then let us both be sudden.
Gon. [*Waking.*]   Now, good angels
Preserve the King ! — [*To* SEBAS. *and* ANTO.]   Why,
     how now ! — [*To* ALON.]   Ho, awake ! —
[*To* SEBAS. *and* ANTO.]   Why are you drawn ? where-
     fore this ghastly looking ? [84]
Alon. [*Waking.*]   What's the matter ?
Seb. Whiles we stood here securing your repose,
Even now, we heard a hollow burst of bellowing
Like bulls, or rather lions : did't not wake you ?
It struck mine ear most terribly.
Alon.   I heard nothing.
Ant. O, 'twas a din to fright a monster's ear,
To make an earthquake ! sure, it was the roar
Of a whole herd of lions.
Alon.   Heard you this, Gonzalo ?
Gon. Upon mine honour, sir, I heard a humming,
And that a strange one too, which did awake me :
I shak'd you, sir, and cried : as mine eyes open'd,
I saw their weapons drawn : — there was a noise,
That's verity. 'Tis best we stand upon our guard,
Or that we quit this place : let's draw our weapons.
Alon. Lead off this ground ; and let's make further
     search
For my poor son.
Gon.   Heavens keep him from these beasts !
For he is, sure, i' the island.
Alon.   Lead away.
                        [*Exit with the others.*

" They'll fall in with any temptation to villainy " ; *they* referring to the other
lords present.

[84] I here give Mr. Dyce's arrangement of the text. In the original the
passage is so printed as to stand in no keeping or coherence with what
follows.

Ari. Prospero my lord shall know what I have
    done : —
So, King, go safely on to seek thy son.   [*Exit.*

SCENE II. *Another part of the Island.*

Enter CALIBAN, *with a burden of Wood. A noise
of Thunder heard.*

Cal. All the infections that the Sun sucks up
From bogs, fens, flats, on Prosper fall, and make him
By inch-meal a disease! His spirits hear me,
And yet I needs must curse. But they'll nor pinch,
Fright me with urchin-shows,[1] pitch me i' the mire,
Nor lead me, like a fire-brand, in the dark
Out of my way, unless he bid 'em : but
For every trifle are they set upon me ;
Sometime like apes, that mow [2] and chatter at me,
And after bite me ; then like hedgehogs, which
Lie tumbling in my barefoot way, and mount
Their pricks [3] at my foot-fall ; sometime am I
All wound with adders, who with cloven tongues
Do hiss me into madness. — Lo, now, lo !
Here comes a spirit of his ; and to torment me
For bringing wood in slowly : I'll fall flat ;
Perchance he will not mind me.

Enter TRINCULO.

Trin. Here's neither bush nor shrub, to bear off any
weather at all, and another storm brewing ; I hear it sing
i' the wind : yond same black cloud, yond huge one, looks
like a foul bumbard [4] that would shed his liquor. If it
should thunder as it did before, I know not where to
hide my head : yond same cloud cannot choose but fall
by pailfuls. — What have we here ? a man or a fish ?
Dead or alive ? A fish : he smells like a fish ; a very ancient and fish-like smell ; a kind of not-of-the-newest
Poor-John.[5] A strange fish ! Were I in England now,
as once I was, and had but this fish painted, not a holiday fool there but would give a piece of silver : there

---

[1] *Urchin-shows* are fairy-shows; as *urchin* was the name of a certain class
of fairies. See page 22, note 44.
[2] To *mow* is to *make mouths.* So Nash's *Pierce Penniless:* "Nobody at
home but an ape, that sat in the porch, and made mops and *mows* at him."
[3] *Pricks* is the ancient word for *prickles.*
[4] A *bumbard* is a black jack of leather, to hold beer, &c.
[5] *Poor-John* is an old name for *hake* salted and dried.

would this monster make a man; any strange beast
there makes a man:[6] when they will not give a doit to
relieve a lame beggar, they will lay out ten to see a dead
Indian.   Legg'd like a man! and his fins like arms!
Warm, o' my troth!   I do now let loose my opinion, hold
it no longer, — this is no fish, but an islander, that hath
lately suffered by a thunderbolt. [*Thunder.*] Alas, the
storm has come again! my best way is to creep under his
gaberdine;[7] there is no other shelter hereabout: misery
acquaints a man with strange bed-fellows. I will here
shroud, till the dregs of the storm be past.

[Creeps under Caliban's Garment.

Enter STEPHANO, singing; a Bottle in his hand.

Ste.   *I shall no more to sea, to sea,*
     Here shall I die ashore; —

This is a very scurvy tune to sing at a man's funeral:
well, here's my comfort.   [*Drinks.*

[*Sings.*] *The master, the swabber, the boatswain, and I,*
         The gunner, and his mate,
     Lov'd Mall, Meg, and Marian, and Margery,
         But none of us car'd for Kate;
         For she had a tongue with a tang,
         Would cry to a sailor, Go hang!
     She lov'd not the savour of tar nor of pitch:
         Then to sea, boys, and let her go hang!

This is a scurvy tune too: but here's my comfort.

[*Drinks.*

Cal. Do not torment me: — O!
Ste. What's the matter? Have we devils here? Do
you put tricks upon's with savages and men of Inde, ha?[8]
I have not scap'd drowning, to be afeard now of your
four legs; for it hath been said, As proper a man as ever
went on four legs cannot make him give ground; and it
shall be said so again, while Stephano breathes at's nos-
trils.

---

[6] Sets a man up, or *makes his fortune*. The phrase was often used thus.
So in *A Midsummer-Night's Dream*, iv. 2: "If our sport had gone forward,
we had all been *made men*."

[7] A *gaberdine* was a coarse outer garment. "A shepherd's pelt, frock,
or *gaberdine*, such a coarse long jacket as our porters wear over the rest of
their garments," says Cotgrave. "A kind of rough cassock or frock like
an Irish mantle," says Philips.

[8] Alluding, probably, to the impostures practised by showmen, who often
played the Barnum with sham wonders pretended to be fetched from
America.

Cal. The spirit torments me : — O !

Ste. This is some monster of the isle with four legs, who hath got, as I take it, an ague. Where the Devil should he learn our language? I will give him some relief, if it be but for that. If I can recover him, and keep him tame, and get to Naples with him, he's a present for any emperor that ever trod on neat's leather.

Cal. Do not torment me, pr'ythee : I'll bring my wood home faster.

Ste. He's in his fit now, and does not talk after the wisest. He shall taste of my bottle : if he have never drunk wine afore, it will go near to remove his fit. If I can recover him, and keep him tame, I will not take too much for him :[9] he shall pay for him that hath him, and that soundly.

Cal. Thou dost me yet but little hurt;
Thou wilt anon, I know it by thy trembling :
Now Prosper works upon thee.

Ste. Come on your ways; open your mouth; here is that which will give language to you, cat : open your mouth; this will shake your shaking, I can tell you, and that soundly : [*Gives him Drink.*] you cannot tell who's your friend; open your chaps again.

[*Gives him more Drink.*

Trin. I should know that voice : it should be — but he is drown'd; and these are devils : — O, defend me !

Ste. Four legs, and two voices, — a most delicate monster ! His forward voice now is to speak well of his friend; his backward voice is to utter foul speeches and to detract. If all the wine in my bottle will recover him, I will help his ague : [*Gives him Drink.*] — Come, — Amen ! I will pour some in thy other mouth.

Trin. Stephano ! —

Ste. Doth thy other mouth call me? Mercy, mercy! This is a devil, and no monster : I will leave him; I have no long spoon.[10]

Trin. Stephano ! — If thou beest Stephano, touch me, and speak to me; for I am Trinculo, — be not afeard, — thy good friend Trinculo.

Ste. If thou beest Trinculo, come forth : I'll pull thee by the lesser legs : if any be Trinculo's legs, these are they. [*Pulls* TRINCULO *out.*] Thou art very Trinculo in-

---

[9] A piece of vulgar irony, meaning, I'll take as much as I can get.

[10] Shakespeare gives his characters appropriate language: "They belch forth proverbs in their drink," "Good honor will *make a out speak*," and "He who eats with the devil had need of *a long spoon.*"

deed! How cam'st thou to be the siege of this moon-calf?[11]

Trin. I took him to be kill'd with a thunder-stroke. — But art thou not drown'd, Stephano? I hope, now, thou art not drown'd? Is the storm overblown? I hid me under the dead moon-calf's gaberdine for fear of the storm. And art thou living, Stephano? O Stephano, two Neapolitans scap'd!

Ste. Pr'ythee, do not turn me about; my stomach is not constant.

Cal. [*Aside.*] These be fine things, an if they be not sprites.
That's a brave god, and bears celestial liquor:
I will kneel to him.

Ste. How didst thou scape? How cam'st thou hither? swear, by this bottle, how thou cam'st hither. I escap'd upon a butt of sack, which the sailors heaved o'erboard, by this bottle! which I made of the bark of a tree with mine own hands, since I was cast ashore.

Cal. I'll swear, upon that bottle, to be thy
True subject; for the liquor is not earthly.

Ste. Here; swear, then, how thou escap'dst.

Trin. Swam ashore, man, like a duck: I can swim like a duck, I'll be sworn.

Ste. Here, kiss the book: [*Gives him Drink.*] Though thou canst swim like a duck, thou art made like a goose.

Trin. O Stephano, hast any more of this?

Ste. The whole butt, man: my cellar is in a rock by the sea-side, where my wine is hid. — How now, moon-calf! how does thine ague?

Cal. Hast thou not dropp'd from heaven?

Ste. Out o' the Moon, I do assure thee: I was the Man-i'-the-moon when time was.

Cal. I've seen thee in her, and I do adore thee:
My mistress show'd me thee, and thy dog, and thy bush.

Ste. Come, swear to that; kiss the book: I will furnish it anon with new contents : — swear.
[*Gives* CALIBAN *Drink.*

Trin. By this good light, this is a very shallow monster! — I afeard of him! — a very weak monster! —

---

[11] *Siege* is an old word for *seat.* So in *Measure for Measure*, iv. 2: "Upon the very *siege* of justice." And in *The Faerie Queene*, ii. 7, 44:

> "A stately *siege* of soveraine majestre,
> And thereon satt a Woman gorgeous gay."

Moon-calf was an imaginary monster, supposed to be generated or misshapen through lunar influence.

The Man-i'-the-moon! — a most poor credulous monster!
— Well drawn, monster, in good sooth.

Cal. I'll show thee every fertile inch o' the island;
And I will kiss thy foot: I pr'ythee, be my god.

Trin. By this light, a most perfidious and drunken
monster! when his god's asleep, he'll rob his bottle.

Cal. I'll kiss thy foot; I'll swear myself thy subject.

Ste. Come on then; down, and swear.

Trin. I shall laugh myself to death at this puppy-
headed monster: a most scurvy monster! I could find
in my heart to beat him, —

Ste. Come, kiss.   [*Gives* Caliban *Drink.*

Trin. — but that the poor monster's in drink: an
abominable monster!

Cal. I'll show thee the best springs; I'll pluck thee
           berries;
I'll fish for thee, and get thee wood enough.
A plague upon the tyrant that I serve!
I'll bear him no more sticks, but follow thee,
Thou wondrous man.

Trin. A most ridiculous monster! to make a wonder
of a poor drunkard.

Cal. I pr'ythee, let me bring thee where crabs grow;
And I with my long nails will dig thee pig-nuts;
Show thee a jay's nest, and instruct thee how
To snare the nimble marmozet: I'll bring thee
To clustering filberds, and sometimes I'll get thee
Young scamels [12] from the rock. Wilt thou go with me?

Ste. I pr'ythee now, lead the way, without any more
talking. — Trinculo, the King and all our company else
being drown'd, we will inherit here. Here, bear my
bottle: fellow Trinculo, we'll fill him by-and-by again.

Cal. [*Sings drunkenly.*] *Farewell, master ; farewell,*
           farewell !

Trin. A howling monster; a drunken monster!

Cal. No more dams I'll make for fish ;
           Nor fetch in firing at requiring ;

---

[12] The original has *scamels* in this place, — a word that has not been found
any where else; though Holt, writing in 1749, says limpets are called *scams*
in some parts of England, and Mr. Halliwell says he has the authority of
Mr. Crofton Croker for asserting, that the term is still used in that sense in
Ireland. Theobald altered *scamels* into *sea-mells;* wherein he has been fol-
lowed by some of the best editions. The sea-mell, or sea-mall, is a species
of gull, which builds its nest in the rock, and which, when young, was
accounted a good dish at the best tables. Dyce thinks *staniel* to be the right
word. Staniel is a species of mountain hawk, and the word is so used in
Twelfth Night. See vol. i. page 207, note 14.

Nor scrape trencher, nor wash dish :
    'Ban, 'Ban, Ca — Caliban
    Has a new master — Get a new man.

Freedom, hey-day ! hey-day, freedom ! freedom, hey-day,
    freedom !
Ste. O brave monster ! lead the way.   [*Exeunt.*

ACT III. Scene I. *Before* Prospero's *Cell.*

Enter Ferdinand, *bearing a Log.*

Ferd. There be some sports are painful, and their labour
Delight in them sets off :[1] some kinds of baseness
Are nobly undergone ; and most poor matters
Point to rich ends. This my mean task
Would be as heavy to me as 'tis odious, but
The mistress which I serve quickens what's dead,
And makes my labours pleasures : O, she is
Ten times more gentle than her father's crabbed,
And he's compos'd of harshness. I must remove
Some thousands of these logs, and pile them up,
Upon a sore injunction : my sweet mistress
Weeps when she sees me work ; and says such baseness
Had never like executor. I forget :
But these sweet thoughts do even refresh my labour,
Most busiest, when I do it.[2]

Enter Miranda ; *and* Prospero *behind.*

Mira.   Alas, now, pray you,
Work not so hard : I would the lightning had
Burnt up those logs that you're enjoin'd to pile !
Pray, set it down, and rest you : when this burns,
'Twill weep for having wearied you. My father
Is hard at study ; pray now, rest yourself :
He's safe for these three hours.

---

[1] The delight we take in those painful sports *offsets* or compensates the
exertion they put us to. A similar thought occurs in *Macbeth :* " The labour
we delight in physics pain."

[2] These sweet thoughts being busiest while I am doing the work. This
doubling of the superlative is very common in all the writers of Shakespeare's time. The original has " most *busie lest* "; which has been a
standing puzzle to the editors. The emendation in the text is Holt White's ;
and I fail to appreciate any of the objections that have been urged against
it. Various other changes have been proposed, but they all seem wide of
the mark, while this is quite satisfactory.

Ferd.   O most dear mistress,
The Sun will set before I shall discharge
What I must strive to do.
Mira.   If you'll sit down,
I'll bear your logs the while : pray, give me that ;
I'll carry't to the pile.
Ferd.   No, precious creature ;
I'd rather crack my sinews, break my back,
Than you should such dishonour undergo,
While I sit lazy by.
Mira.   It would become me
As well as it does you : and I should do it
With much more ease ; for my good will is to it,
And yours 'tis 'gainst.
Pros. [*Aside.*]   Poor worm, thou art infected !
This visitation shows it.
Mira.   You look wearily.
Ferd. No, noble mistress ; 'tis fresh morning with
      me
When you are by at night. I do beseech you, —
Chiefly that I might set it in my prayers, —
What is your name ?
Mira.   Miranda : — O my father,
I've broke your hest to say so !
Ferd.   Admir'd Miranda !
Indeed the top of admiration ; worth
What's dearest to the world ! Full many a lady
I've ey'd with best regard ; and many a time
The harmony of their tongues hath into bondage
Brought my too diligent ear : for several virtues
Have I lik'd several women ; never any
With so full soul, but some defect in her
Did quarrel with the noblest grace she ow'd,
And put it to the foil : but you, O you,
So perfect and so peerless, are created
Of every creature's best !
Mira.   I do not know
One of my sex ; no woman's face remember,
Save, from my glass, mine own ; nor have I seen
More that I may call men, than you, good friend,
And my dear father: how features are abroad,
I'm skill-less of ; but, by my modesty, —
The jewel in my dower, — I would not wish
Any companion in the world but you ;
Nor can imagination form a shape,
Besides yourself, to like of. But I prattle

Something too wildly, and my father's precepts
I therein do forget.
  Ferd.   I am, in my condition,
A prince, Miranda; I do think, a king, —
I would, not so! — and would no more endure
This wooden slavery than to suffer
The flesh-fly blow my mouth. Hear my soul speak:
The very instant that I saw you, did
My heart fly to your service; there resides,
To make me slave to it; and for your sake
Am I this patient log-man.
  Mira.   Do you love me?
  Ferd. O Heaven, O Earth, bear witness to this sound,
And crown what I profess with kind event,
If I speak true! if hollowly, invert
What best is boded me to mischief! I,
Beyond all limit of what else[3] i' the world,
Do love, prize, honour you.
  Mira.   I am a fool
To weep at what I'm glad of.
  Pros. [*Aside.*]   Fair encounter
Of two most rare affections! Heavens rain grace
On that which breeds between them!
  Ferd.   Wherefore weep you?
  Mira. At mine unworthiness, that dare not offer
What I desire to give; and much less take
What I shall die to want. But this is trifling;
And all the more it seeks to hide itself,
The bigger bulk it shows. Hence, bashful cunning!
And prompt me, plain and holy innocence!
I am your wife, if you will marry me;
If not, I'll die your maid: to be your fellow
You may deny me; but I'll be your servant,
Whether you will or no.
  Ferd.   My mistress, dearest,
And I thus humble ever.
  Mira.   My husband, then?
  Ferd. Ay, with a heart as willing
As bondage e'er of freedom: here's my hand.
  Mira. And mine, with my heart in't: and now fare-
   well,
Till half an hour hence.
  Ferd.   A thousand thousand![4]
        [*Exeunt* FERD. *and* MIR.

---

[3] *What* else, for *whatsoever* else.
[4] Evidently a thousand thousand farewells.

Pros. So glad of this as they, I cannot be,
Who are surpris'd withal; but my rejoicing
At nothing can be more. I'll to my book;
For yet, ere supper-time, must I perform
Much business appertaining.   [*Exit.*

Scene II. *Another part of the Island.*

Enter Caliban, Stephano, *and* Trinculo, *with a Bottle.*

Ste. Tell not me;—when the butt is out, we will
drink water; not a drop before: therefore bear up, and
board 'em.—Servant-monster, drink to me.

Trin. Servant-monster! the folly of this island! They
say there's but five upon this isle: we are three of them;
if th' other two be brain'd like us, the State totters.

Ste. Drink, servant-monster, when I bid thee: thy
eyes are almost set in thy head.·   [Caliban *drinks.*

Trin. Where should they be set else? he were a brave
monster indeed, if they were set in his tail.

Ste. My man-monster hath drown'd his tongue in
sack: for my part, the sea cannot drown me; I swam, ere
I could recover the shore, five-and-thirty leagues, off and
on, by this light.—Thou shalt be my lieutenant, monster,
or my standard.[1]

Trin. Your lieutenant, if you list; he's no standard.

Ste. We'll not run, Monsieur Monster.

Trin. Nor go neither: but you'll lie like dogs, and
yet say nothing neither.

Ste. Moon-calf, speak once in thy life, if thou beest a
good moon-calf.

Cal. How does thy honour? Let me lick thy shoe.
I'll not serve him, he is not valiant.

Trin. Thou liest, most ignorant monster: I am in case
to justle a constable. Why, thou debosh'd[2] fish, thou,
was there ever man a coward that hath drunk so much
sack as I to-day? Wilt thou tell a monstrous lie, being
but half a fish and half a monster?

Cal. Lo, how he mocks me! wilt thou let him, my lord?

Trin. *Lord,* quoth he!—that a monster should be
such a natural![3]

Cal. Lo, lo, again! bite him to death, I pr'ythee.

Ste. Trinculo, keep a good tongue in your head: if

---

[1] *Standard* is standard-*bearer*, or *ensign.*
[2] *Deboshed* is the old orthography of *debauched.* ·
[3] *Natural* was used for *simpleton* or *fool.* See vol. i. page 29, note 4.
There is also a quibble intended between *monster* and *natural,* a monster
being *unnatural.*

you prove a mutineer, — the next tree. The poor monster's my subject, and he shall not suffer indignity.

Cal. I thank my noble lord. Wilt thou be pleas'd
To hearken once again the suit I made thee?

Ste. Marry, will I : kneel, and repeat it; I will stand,
and so shall Trinculo.

Enter ARIEL, *invisible.*

Cal. As I told thee before, I am subject to a tyrant;
a sorcerer, that by his cunning hath cheated me of the
island.

Ari. Thou liest.

Cal. Thou liest, thou jesting monkey, thou.
I would my valiant master would destroy thee!
I do not lie.

Ste. Trinculo, if you trouble him any more in's tale,
by this hand, I will supplant some of your teeth.

Trin. Why, I said nothing.

Ste. Mum, then, and no more. — [*To* CAL.] Proceed.

Cal. I say, by sorcery he got this isle;
From me he got it. If thy Greatness will
Revenge it on him, — for, I know, thou dar'st,
But this thing dare not, —

Ste. That's most certain.

Cal. — Thou shalt be lord of it, and I will serve thee.

Ste. How now shall this be compass'd? Canst thou
bring me to the party?

Cal. Yea, yea, my lord; I'll yield him thee asleep,
Where thou may'st knock a nail into his head.

Ari. Thou liest; thou canst not.

Cal. What a pied ninny's this![4] — Thou scurvy
patch ! —
I do beseech thy Greatness, give him blows,
And take his bottle from him : when that's gone,
He shall drink nought but brine; for I'll not show him
Where the quick freshes [5] are.

Ste. Trinculo, run into no further danger: interrupt
the monster one word further, and, by this hand, I'll
turn my mercy out of doors, and make a stock-fish of thee.

Trin. Why, what did I? I did nothing : I'll go
further off.

Ste. Didst thou not say he lied?

---

[4] *Pied* is *dappled* or *diversely-coloured.* Trinculo is "an allowed Fool" or
jester, and wears a motley dress. *Patch* refers to the same circumstance.
See vol. i. page 124, note 8.

[5] *Quick freshes* are *living springs.*

Ari. Thou liest.

Ste. Do I so? take thou that. [*Strikes him.*] As you like this, give me the lie another time.

Trin. I did not give thee the lie : — Out o' your wits and hearing too? — A pox o' your bottle! this can sack and drinking do. — A murrain on your monster, and the Devil take your fingers!

Cal. Ha, ha, ha!

Ste. Now, forward with your tale. — Pr'ythee stand further off.

Cal. Beat him enough : after a little time, I'll beat him too.

Ste. Stand further. — Come, proceed.

Cal. Why, as I told thee, 'tis a custom with him
I' the afternoon to sleep : then thou may'st brain him,
Having first seiz'd his books ; or with a log
Batter his skull, or paunch him with a stake,
Or cut his wezand [6] with thy knife. Remember,
First to possess his books ; for without them
He's but a sot,[7] as I am, nor hath not
One spirit to command : they all do hate him,
As rootedly as I : burn but his books.
He has brave utensils, — for so he calls them, —
Which, when he has a house, he'll deck't withal :
And that most deeply to consider is
The beauty of his daughter ; he himself
Calls her a nonpareil : I ne'er saw woman,
But only Sycorax my dam and she ;
But she as far surpasseth Sycorax
As great'st does least.

Ste.   Is it so brave a lass?

Cal. Ay, lord.

Ste. Monster, I will kill this man : his daughter and I will be king and queen, — save our Graces! and Trinculo and thyself shall be viceroys. — Dost thou like the plot, Trinculo?

Trin. Excellent.

Ste. Give me thy hand ; I am sorry I beat thee : but, while thou livest, keep a good tongue in thy head.

Cal. Within this half-hour will he be asleep :
Wilt thou destroy him then?

Ste. Ay, on mine honour.

Ari. This will I tell my master.

---

[6] *Wezand* is *throat* or *windpipe.*

[7] *Sot*, from the French, was often used for *fool; as* our word *besotted* sometimes is. See vol. i. page 187, note 12.

Cal. Thou mak'st me merry: I am full of pleasure.
Let us be jocund : will you troll the catch
You taught me but while-ere ?

Ste. At thy request, monster, I will do reason, any
reason :— Come on, Trinculo, let us sing.   [*Sings.*

*Flout 'em and scout 'em, and scout 'em and flout 'em ;
Thought is free.*

Cal. That's not the tune.

          [ARIEL *plays the tune on a Tabor and Pipe.*
Ste. What is this same ?

Trin. This is the tune of our catch, play'd by the
picture of Nobody.[8]

Ste. If thou beest a man, show thyself in thy likeness :
if thou beest a devil, take't as thou list.

Trin. O, forgive me my sins !

Ste. He that dies pays all debts : I defy thee. — Mercy
upon us !

Cal. Art thou afeard ?

Ste. No, monster, not I.

Cal. Be not afeard ; the isle is full of noises,
Sounds and sweet airs that give delight and hurt not.
Sometime a thousand twangling instruments
Will hum about mine ears ; and sometime voices,
That, if I then had wak'd after long sleep,
Will make me sleep again : and then, in dreaming,
The clouds methought would open, and show riches
Ready to drop upon me ; that, when I wak'd,
I cry'd to dream again.

Ste. This will prove a brave kingdom to me, where I
shall have my music for nothing.

Cal. When Prospero is destroy'd.

Ste. That shall be by-and-by : I remember the story.

Trin. The sound is going away ; let's follow it, and
after do our work.

Ste. Lead, monster ; we'll follow. — I would I could
see this taborer :[9] he lays it on. — Wilt come ?

Trin. I'll follow, Stephano.   [*Exeunt.*

---

[8] *The picture of Nobody* was a common sign, and consisted of a head upon
two legs, with arms. There was also a wood-cut prefixed to an old play of
Nobody and Somebody, which represented this personage.

[9] You shall heare in the ayre the sound of *tabers and other instruments*, to
put the travellers in feare, by evill spirites that makes these soundes, and
also do call diverse of the travellers by their names. *Travels of Marcus
Paulus*, 1579. To some of these circumstances Milton also alludes:

> " Of calling shapes, and beckoning shadows dire ;
>   And aery tongues that syllable men's names
>   On sands, and shores, and desert wildernesses."

SCENE III. *Another part of the Island.*

Enter ALONSO, SEBASTIAN, ANTONIO, GONZALO, ADRIAN,
FRANCISCO, *and others.*

Gon. By'r lakin,[1] I can go no further, sir;
My old bones ache: here's a maze trod, indeed,
Through forth-rights and meanders![2] by your patience,
I needs must rest me.
 Alon.   Old lord, I cannot blame thee,
Who am myself attach'd with weariness,
To th' dulling of my spirits: sit down, and rest.
Even here I will put off my hope, and keep it
No longer for my flatterer: he is drown'd
Whom thus we stray to find; and the sea mocks
Our frustrate search on land. Well, let him go.
 Ant. [*Aside to* SEB.] I am right glad that he's so out
  of hope.
Do not, for one repulse, forego the purpose
That you resolv'd t' effect.
 Seb. [*Aside to* ANT.] The next advantage
Will we take throughly.
 Ant. [*Aside to* SEB.] Let it be to-night;
For, now they are oppress'd with travel, they
Will not, nor cannot, use such vigilance
As when they 're fresh.
 Seb. [*Aside to* ANT.] I say, to-night; no more.
        [*Solemn and strange Music.*
 Alon. What harmony is this? — My good friends,
  hark!
 Gon. Marvellous sweet music!

Enter PROSPERO, *above, invisible. Enter, below, several
strange Shapes, bringing in a Banquet: they dance
about it with gentle actions of salutation; and, invit-
ing the* KING, *&c., to eat, they depart.*

 Alon. Give us kind keepers, Heavens! — What were
  these?
 Seb. A living drollery.[3] Now I will believe
That there are unicorns; that in Arabia

---

 [1] *By'r lakin* is a contraction of *By our ladykin*, the diminutive of *our
Lady.*
 [2] *Forth-rights* means straight lines; *meanders*, crooked ones.
 [3] Shows, called *Drolleries*, were in Shakespeare's time performed by
puppets only. "A living drollery" is therefore a drollery not by wooden
but by living personages.

There is one tree, the phœnix' throne; [4] one phœnix
At this hour reigning there.
    Ant.   I'll believe both;
And what does else want credit, come to me,
And I'll be sworn 'tis true : travellers ne'er did lie,
Though fools at home condemn 'em.
    Gon.   If in Naples
I should report this now, would they believe me?
If I should say I saw such islanders,
(For, certes,[5] these are people of the island,)
Who, though they are of monstrous shape, yet, note,
Their manners are more gentle-kind than of
Our human generation you shall find
Many, nay, almost any.
    Pros. [*Aside.*]   Honest lord,
Thou hast said well; for some of you there present
Are worse than devils.
    Alon.   I cannot too much muse,[6]
Such shapes, such gesture, and such sound, expressing —
Although they want the use of tongue — a kind
Of excellent dumb discourse.
    Pros. [*Aside.*]   Praise in departing.[7]
    Fran. They vanish'd strangely.
    Seb.   No matter, since
They've left their viands behind; for we have stomachs. —
Will't please you taste of what is here?
    Alon.   Not I.
    Gon. Faith, sir, you need not fear. When we were boys,
Who would believe that there were mountaineers
Dew-lapp'd like bulls, whose throats had hanging at 'em
Wallets of flesh? or that there were such men
Whose heads stood in their breasts? which now we find,
Each putter-out of one [8] for five will bring us
Good warrant of.

---

[4] I myself have heard strange things of this kind of tree; namely, in regard of the bird Phœnix, which is supposed to have taken that name of this date tree (called in Greek φοινιξ); for it was assured unto me, that the said bird died with that tree, and revived of itselfe as the tree sprung againe. — *Holland's Pliny.*

[5] The Poet several times uses *certes* for. *certainly.* The usage was common.

[6] To *muse* is to *wonder;* often so used. See vol. i. page 392, note 13.

[7] *Praise in departing* is a proverbial phrase signifying, Do not praise your entertainment too soon, lest you should have cause to retract.

[8] A sort of inverted life-insurance was practised by travellers in Shakespeare's time. Before going abroad they *put out* a sum of money, for which they were to receive two, three, four, or even five times the amount upon their return; the rate being according to the supposed danger of the expedition. Of course the sum put out fell to the depositary, in case the *putter-*

Alon.   I will stand to, and feed,
Although my last: no matter, since I feel
The best is past. — Brother, my lord the Duke,
Stand to, and do as we.

Thunder and lightning. Enter ARIEL *like a harpy;
claps his wings upon the table, and, by a quaint device,
the banquet vanishes.*

Ari. You are three men of sin, whom Destiny —
That hath to instrument this lower world
And what is in't — the never-surfeited sea
Hath caus'd to belch up you,[9] and on this island
Where man doth not inhabit; you 'mongst men
Being most unfit to live. I've made you mad;
And even with such like valour men hang and drown
Their proper selves.
            [*Seeing* ALON. SEB. *&c. draw their Swords.*
                    You fools! I and my fellows
Are ministers of Fate: the elements,
Of whom your swords are temper'd, may as well
Wound the loud winds, or with bemock'd-at stabs
Kill the still-closing waters, as diminish
One dowle [10] that's in my plume : my fellow ministers
Are like invulnerable. If you could hurt,
Your swords are now too massy for your strengths,
And will not be uplifted. But remember, —
For that's my business to you, — that you three
From Milan did supplant good Prospero ;
Expos'd unto the sea, which hath requit it,
Him and his innocent child : for which foul deed
The powers, delaying, not forgetting, have
Incens'd the seas and shores, yea, all the creatures,
Against your peace. Thee of thy son, Alonso,
They have bereft ; and do pronounce, by me,
Lingering perdition — worse than any death
Can be at once — shall step by step attend
You and your ways ; whose wrath to guard you from, —

out did not return. The men, "whose heads stood in their breasts," were
probably the same that Othello speaks of: "The Anthropophagi, and men
whose heads do grow beneath their shoulders."—The report of "mountaineers dew-lapp'd like bulls" may have sprung from some remarkable cases
of *goître*, seen by travellers, but not understood.

[9] Shakespeare sometimes uses both the relative and the personal pro-
nouns in relative clauses, where, properly, only one of them should have
place; as *whom* and *you* in this instance. See vol. i. page 39, note 2, and
page 112, note 15. Some editors omit *you* in this place, and print *caus'd* a
dissyllable, *caused.*

[10] Bailey, in his *Dictionary*, says that *dowle* is a feather, or rather the
single particles of the down.

Which here, in this most desolate isle, else falls
Upon your heads, — is nothing, but heart's sorrow
And a clear life ensuing.

He vanishes in thunder; then, to soft music, enter the
Shapes again, and dance with mocks and mowes, and
carry out the table.

Pros. [*Aside.*] Bravely the figure of this harpy hast
   thou
Perform'd, my Ariel; a grace it had, devouring:
Of my instruction hast thou nothing 'bated
In what thou hadst to say: so, with good life,[11]
And observation strange, my meaner ministers
Their several kinds have done. My high charms work,
And these mine enemies are all knit up
In their distractions: they now are in my power;
And in these fits I leave them, while I visit
Young Ferdinand, — who they suppose is drown'd, —
And his and my lov'd darling. [*Exit from above.*
Gon. I' the name of something holy, sir, why stand you
In this strange stare?
Alon.   O, it is monstrous, monstrous!
Methought the billows spoke, and told me of it;
The winds did sing it to me; and the thunder,
That deep and dreadful organ pipe, pronounc'd
The name of Prosper: it did bass my trespass.
Therefore my son i' the ooze is bedded; and
I'll seek him deeper than e'er plummet sounded,
And with him there lie mudded.   [*Exit.*
Seb.   But one fiend at a time,
I'll fight their legions o'er.
Ant.   I'll be thy second.
        [*Exeunt* SEB. *and* ANT.
Gon. All three of them are desperate: their great guilt,
Like poison given to work a long time after,[12]
Now 'gins to bite the spirits. — I do beseech you,
That are of suppler joints, follow them swiftly,
And hinder them from what this ecstasy [18]
May now provoke them to.
Adr.   Follow, I pray you.
        [*Exeunt.*

[11] *With good life* probably means the same as our phrase "acted to the
life"; though some explain it "with full bent and energy of mind."
  [12] The natives of Africa have been supposed to possess the secret how to
temper poisons with such art as not to operate till several years after they
were administered.
  [18] Shakespeare uses *ecstasy* for any temporary alienation of mind, a fit or
madness. See vol. i. page 548, note 15.

ACT IV.   SCENE I.   *Before* PROSPERO's *Cell.*

Enter PROSPERO, FERDINAND, *and* MIRANDA.

Pros. If I have too austerely punish'd you,
Your compensation makes amends ;[1] for I
Have given you here a thread of mine own life,[2]
Or that for which I live : who once again
I tender to thy hand : all thy vexations
Were but my trials of thy love, and thou
Hast strangely stood the test : here, afore Heaven,
I ratify this my rich gift.   O Ferdinand,
Do not smile at me that I boast her off,
For thou shalt find she will outstrip all praise,
And make it halt behind her.
     Ferd.   I do believe it
Against an oracle.
     Pros.   Then, as my gift, and thine own acquisition
Worthily purchas'd, take my daughter : but
If thou dost break her virgin knot[3] before
All sanctimonious ceremonies may
With full and holy rite be minister'd,
No sweet aspersion[4] shall the Heavens let fall
To make this contract grow ; but barren hate,
Sour-ey'd disdain, and discord, shall bestrew
The union of your bed with weeds so loathly,
That you shall hate it both : therefore take heed,
As Hymen's lamps shall light you.
     Ferd.   As I hope
For quiet days, fair issue, and long life,
With such love as 'tis now, the strong'st suggestion[5]
Our worser Genius can shall never melt
Mine honour into lust.
     Pros.   Fairly spoke.
Sit, then, and talk with her ; she is thine own. —
What, Ariel ! my industrious servant, Ariel !

Enter ARIEL.

Ari. What would my potent master ? here I am.
Pros. Thou and thy meaner fellows your last service

---

[1] *Your compensation* is the compensation *you receive.* Shakespeare has many instances of like construction.

[2] "Thread of mine own life" probably means about the same as our phrase "my very *heart-strings*"; strings the breaking of which spills the life.

[3] Alluding, no doubt, to the zone or sacred girdle which the old Romans used as the symbol and safeguard of maiden honour.

[4] *Aspersion* is here used in its primitive sense of *sprinkling.*

[5] *Suggestion* here means *temptation* or *wicked prompting.* See page 37, note 33.

Did worthily perform; and I must use you
In such another trick. Go bring the rabble,
O'er whom I give thee power, here, to this place:
Incite them to quick motion; for I must
Bestow upon the eyes of this young couple
Some vanity[6] of mine art: it is my promise,
And they expect it from me.
    Ari.   Presently?
    Pros. Ay, with a twink.
    Ari. Before you can say, *Come*, and *Go*,
And breathe twice, and cry, *So, so*,
Each one, tripping on his toe,
Will be here with mop and mow.[7]
Do you love me, master? — no?
    Pros. Dearly, my delicate Ariel. Do not approach
Till thou dost hear me call.
    Ari.   Well; I conceive.   [*Exit.*
    Pros. Look thou be true: do not give dalliance
Too much the rein; the strongest oaths are straw
To th' fire i' the blood.
    Ferd.   I warrant you, sir:
The white-cold virgin snow upon my heart
Abates the ardour of my liver.[8]
    Pros.   Well. —
Now come, my Ariel! bring a corollary,[9]
Rather than want a spirit: appear, and pertly! —
No tongue, all eyes; be silent.   [*Soft Music.*

Enter IRIS.

    Iris. Ceres, most bounteous lady, thy rich leas
Of wheat, rye, barley, vetches, oats, and peas;
Thy turfy mountains, where live nibbling sheep,
And flat meads thatch'd with stover,[10] them to keep;
Thy banks with peonied and lilied brims,[11]

---

[6] *Vanity*, according to Mr. Dyce, here means "a magical show or illusion."

[7] *Mop* and *mow* were very often used thus together, the two words meaning about the same thing, — *grimacing* and *making mouths*. See page 39, note 2.

[8] The liver was supposed to be the special seat of certain passions, and so was often put for the passions themselves. See vol. i. page 66, note 45, and page 203, note 9.

[9] *Corollary* here means a surplus number; more than enough. — *Pertly*, in the next line, is *nimbly, alertly.*

[10] *Stover* is fodder for cattle, as hay, straw, and such like; still used thus in the north of England.

[11] The original has "*pioned* and *twilled* brims"; which reading some late editors have retained, taking *pioned* to mean *dug*, and *twilled* to mean *ridged*, or made into ridges, a sense which it yet bears in reference to some

Which spongy April at thy hest betrims,
To make cold nymphs chaste crowns; and thy brown
     groves,
Whose shadow the dismissed bachelor loves,
Being lass-lorn;[12] thy pole-clipt vineyard;
And thy sea-marge, steril, and rocky-hard,
Where thou thyself dost air;—the Queen o' the Sky,
Whose watery arch and messenger am I,
Bids thee leave these, and with her sovereign Grace,
Here on this grass-plot, in this very place,
To come and sport. Her peacocks fly amain:
Approach, rich Ceres, her to entertain.

Enter CERES.

Cer. Hail, many-colour'd messenger, that ne'er
Dost disobey the wife of Jupiter;
Who, with thy saffron wings, upon my flowers
Diffusest honey-drops, refreshing showers;
And with each end of thy blue bow dost crown
My bosky acres[13] and my unshrubb'd down,
Rich scarf to my proud earth;—why hath thy Queen
Summon'd me hither, to this short-grass'd green?
Iris. A contract of true love to celebrate;
And some donation freely to estate
On the bless'd lovers.
Cer.   Tell me, heavenly Bow,
If Venus or her son, as thou dost know,
Do now attend the Queen?
Her and her blind boy's scandal'd company
I have forsworn.
Iris.   Of her society
Be not afraid: I met her deity
Cutting the clouds towards Paphos, and her son

kinds of linen. Henley urges in behalf of the old reading, that pionies and lilies never bloom in April; which is refuted by a passage in Lord Bacon's Essay *Of Gardens:* "In April follow the double white violet, the wall-flower, the stock-gilly-flower, the cowslip, flower-de-luces, and *lilies of all natures;* rose-mary flowers, the tulip, the double *piony,* the pale daffodil," &c. But the main objection to the old reading lies in the words, "to make cold nymphs chaste crowns," which apparently refer to the popular belief touching the flowers in question. Lyte, in his *Herbal,* says, "One kind of *peonie* is called by some, *maiden* or *virgin* peonie." And Edward Fenton, in his *Secret Wonders of Nature,* 1569, says, "The water-lily mortifieth altogether the appetite of sensuality, and defends from unchaste thoughts."

[12] *Lass-lorn* is *forsaken by his lass,* the sweet-heart that has *dismissed* him.—*Pole-clipt* is *fenced in* or *enclosed with poles:* or it may mean poles embraced or clasped by the vines; which is Dyce's explanation. *Clip* was often used for *embrace.*

[13] *Bosky acres* are woody acres, fields intersected by luxuriant hedge-rows and copses. See vol. i. page 321, note 1.

3*

Dove-drawn with her: Here thought they to have done
Some wanton charm upon this man and maid.
Her waspish-headed son has broke his arrows,
Swears he will shoot no more, but play with sparrows,
And be a boy right out.
    Cer.   Highest Queen of state,[14]
Great Juno comes; I know her by her gait.

Enter JUNO.

   Juno. How does my bounteous sister?   Go with me
To bless this twain, that they may prosperous be,
And honour'd in their issue.

Song.

   Juno. Honour, riches, marriage-blessing,
       Long continuance, and increasing,
       Hourly joys be still upon you!
       Juno sings her blessings on you.

   Cer. Earth's increase, and foison plenty,
       Barns and garners never empty;
       Vines with clustering bunches growing;
       Plants with goodly burden bowing;
       Spring come to you at the farthest
       In the very end of harvest! [15]
       Scarcity and want shall shun you;
       Ceres' blessing so is on you.

   Ferd. This is a most majestic vision, and
Harmonious charmingly.[16]   May I be bold
To think these spirits?
   Pros.   Spirits, which by mine art
I have from their confines call'd to enact
My present fancies.
   Ferd.   Let me live here ever;
So rare a wonder'd [17] father and a wife
Make this place Paradise.
        [JUNO *and* CERES *whisper, and send* IRIS *on*
           employment.

---

[14] "Highest Queen of state" means the same as Queen of highest state, or Queen above all other queens. Such inversions are frequent; as in second note below.

[15] The meaning seems to be, May your new Spring begin, at the latest, as soon as the harvest of the old one is over.

[16] As we should say, charmingly harmonious.

[17] A father able to work such rare wonders.—The original has *wise* instead of *wife.* As *s* was then commonly written long, it might easily get misprinted for *f.* I can hardly think that Ferdinand would leave the wife out of such a reckoning; especially that wife being Miranda.

Pros.   Sweet, now, silence!
Juno and Ceres whisper seriously;
There's something else to do : hush, and be mute,
Or else our spell is marr'd.[18]
  Iris. You nymphs, call'd Naiads, of the wandering
      brooks,
With your sedge crowns and ever-harmless looks,
Leave your crisp channels,[19] and on this green land
Answer your summons; Juno does command :
Come, temperate nymphs, and help to celebrate
A contract of true love ; be not too late. —

Enter certain Nymphs.

You sun-burn'd sicklemen, of August weary,
Come hither from the furrow, and be merry :
Make holiday; your rye-straw hats put on,
And these fresh nymphs encounter every one
In country footing.

*Enter certain Reapers, properly habited : they join with
    the Nymphs in a graceful dance ; towards the end
    whereof* PROSPERO *starts suddenly, and speaks ; after
    which, to a strange, hollow, and confused noise, they
    heavily vanish.*

  Pros. [*Aside.*] I had forgot that foul conspiracy
Of the beast Caliban and his confederates
Against my life : the minute of their plot
Is almost come. — [*To the Spirits.*] Well done; — avoid;
      — no more.
  Ferd. This is most strange : your father's in some
      passion
That works him strongly.
  Mira.   Never till this day
Saw I him touch'd with anger so distemper'd.
  Pros. Sure, you do look, my son, in a mov'd sort,
As if you were dismay'd : be cheerful, sir.
Our revels now are ended.   These our actors,
As I foretold you, were all spirits, and
Are melted into air, into thin air :

---

   [18] It was supposed that any noise or disturbance would upset or discon-
cert "the might of magic spells."
   [19] *Crisp* is *curled*, from the curl made by a breeze on the surface of the
water. See vol. i. page 263, note 11. The transference of an epithet to an
associated object, as of *crisp* from the water to the channel in this instance,
is one of Shakespeare's favourite traits of style. So in *Romeo and Juliet*,
iii. 5, when the lovers see tokens of the dawn that is to *sever* them, Romeo
says, "what envious streaks do lace the *severing clouds* in yonder east."

And, like the baseless fabric of this vision,
The cloud-capp'd towers, the gorgeous palaces,
The solemn temples, the great globe itself,
Yea, all which it inherit, shall dissolve;
And, like this insubstantial pageant faded,[20]
Leave not a wreck behind.   We are such stuff
As dreams are made on, and our little life
Is rounded with a sleep. — Sir, I am vex'd;
Bear with my weakness; my old brain is troubled:
Be not disturb'd with my infirmity.
If you be pleas'd, retire into my cell,
And there repose: a turn or two I'll walk,
To still my beating mind.
  Ferd. Mira.   We wish you peace.
  Pros. [*To* ARIEL.] Come with a thought!—I thank
   ye. [*Exeunt* FERD. *and* MIRA.]—Ariel, come![21]

Re-enter ARIEL.

  Ari. Thy thoughts I cleave to: what's thy pleasure?
  Pros.   Spirit,
We must prepare to meet with Caliban.[22]
  Ari. Ay, my commander: when I presented Ceres,
I thought t' have told thee of it; but I fear'd
Lest I might anger thee.
  Pros. Say again, where didst thou leave these varlets?
  Ari. I told you, sir, they were red-hot with drinking;
So full of valour, that they smote the air
For breathing in their faces; beat the ground
For kissing of their feet; yet always bending
Towards their project.   Then I beat my tabor;
At which, like unback'd colts, they prick'd their ears,
Advanc'd their eyelids, lifted up their noses
As they smelt music: so I charm'd their ears,
That, calf-like, they my lowing follow'd through
Tooth'd briers, sharp furzes, pricking goss, and thorns,
Which enter'd their frail shins: at last I left them

---

[20] *Faded,* from the Latin *vado,* is the same as *vanished. — Inherit* was often used in the sense of *possess.*

[21] The words "I thank ye" are addressed to Ferdinand and Miranda in return for their "We wish you peace."   Instead of *ye* the original has *thee,* which makes Prospero thank Ariel.   It does not well appear why he should thus be thanking Ariel: I therefore adopt the reading and arrangement of Mr. Dyce.

[22] *To meet with* was anciently the same as to *counteract* or *oppose.*   So in Herbert's *Country Parson:* "He knows the temper and pulse of every one in his house, and accordingly either *meets with* their vices, or advanceth their virtues."

I' the filthy-mantled pool beyond your cell,
There dancing up to th' chins.
 Pros.   This was well done, my bird.
Thy shape invisible retain thou still :
The trumpery in my house, go bring it hither,
For stale [23] to catch these thieves.
 Ari.   I go, I go.   [*Exit.*
 Pros. A devil, a born devil, on whose nature
Nurture can never stick ; [24] on whom my pains,
Humanely taken, all are lost, quite lost ;
And as with age his body uglier grows,
So his mind cankers. [25] I will plague them all,

  Re-enter ARIEL *loaden with glistering Apparel, &c.*

Even to roaring. — Come, hang them on this line.

PROSPERO *and* ARIEL *remain, invisible.* *Enter* CALIBAN,
  STEPHANO, *and* TRINCULO, *all wet.*

 Cal. Pray you, tread softly, that the blind mole may
   not
Hear a foot fall : we now are near his cell.
 Ste. Monster, your fairy, which you say is a harmless
fairy, has done little better than play'd the Jack with us. [26]
 Trin. Monster, I do smell all [stench here] ; at which
my nose is in great indignation.
 Ste. So is mine. — Do you hear, monster ? If I should
take a displeasure against you, look you, —
 Trin. Thou wert but a lost monster.
 Cal. Good my lord, give me thy favour still.
Be patient, for the prize I'll bring thee to
Shall hood-wink this mischance : therefore speak softly ; —
All's hush'd as midnight yet.
 Trin. Ay, but to lose our bottles in the pool, —
 Ste. There is not only disgrace and dishonour in that,
monster, but an infinite loss.

 [23] *Stale,* in the art of fowling, signified a *bait* or *lure* to decoy birds.
 [24] *Nurture* is *culture, education.* See vol. i. page 51, note 14.
 [25] *Canker* was used of an *eating,* malignant sore, like *cancer,* which is
indeed but another form of the same word. It was also used of *rust ;* as in
St. James, v. 3 : " Your gold and silver is *cankered ;* and the *rust* of them
shall be a witness against you." I am not quite certain which of these
senses it bears here ; probably the first. Shakespeare has the word repeatedly in both senses ; as in *Romeo and Juliet,* i. 1, where the first *canker'd*
means *rusted,* while the second has the sense of *cancer :*
   " To wield old partizans, in hands as old,
    Canker'd with peace, to part your *canker'd* hate."
 [26] To play the *Jack,* was to play the *Knave ;* or it may have been, to play
the *Jack-o'-lantern,* by leading them astray.

Trin. That's more to me than my wetting: yet this is your harmless fairy, monster.

Ste. I will fetch off my bottle, though I be o'er ears for my labour.

Cal. Pr'ythee, my King, be quiet.   Seest thou here? This is the mouth o' the cell: no noise, and enter. Do that good mischief which may make this island Thine own for ever, and I, thy Caliban, For aye thy foot-licker.

Ste. Give me thy hand: I do begin to have bloody thoughts.

Trin. O King Stephano! O peer![27] O worthy Stephano! look, what a wardrobe here is for thee!

Cal. Let it alone, thou fool; it is but trash.

Trin. O, ho, monster! we know what belongs to a frippery.[28] — O King Stephano!

Ste. Put off that gown, Trinculo: by this hand, I'il have that gown.

Trin. Thy Grace shall have it.

Cal. The dropsy drown this fool! — what do you mean, To dote thus on such luggage?   Let's along, And do the murder first: if he awake, From toe to crown he'll fill our skins with pinches; Make us strange stuff.

Ste. Be you quiet, monster. — Mistress line, is not this my jerkin? Now is the jerkin under the line: now, jerkin, you are like to lose your hair, and prove a bald jerkin.[29]

Trin. Do, do: we steal by line and level, an't like your Grace.

Ste. I thank thee for that jest; here's a garment for't: wit shall not go unrewarded while I am king of this country. *Steal by line and level* is an excellent pass of pate;[30] there's another garment for't.

Trin. Monster, come, put some lime upon your fingers,[31] and away with the rest.

[27] This is a humourous allusion to the old ballad "King Stephen was a worthy peer," of which Iago sings a verse in *Othello*.

[28] A shop for the sale of old clothes.

[29] King Stephano quibbles rather superlatively here. To make his wit intelligible it must be noted that the clothes-line is supposed to be made of *hair*, and that a loss of hair was sometimes caused by fevers in tropical regions, or under the equinoctial-*line*. *Jerkin* was the name of a man's upper garment. — *Do, do*, in the next speech, is said in approval of Stephano's wit. — "Steal by line and level" is a further punning on the clothes-line: the plumb-line and the level being instruments used by architects and builders.

[30] *Pass of pate* is a *spurt* or *sally of wit;* *pass* being, in the language of fencing, a *thrust*.

[31] *Lime*, or *bird-lime*, was a sticky substance used for catching birds. See vol. i. page 220, note 4, and page 586, note 5.

Cal. I will have none on't : we shall lose our time,
And all be turn'd to barnacles,[82] or apes
With foreheads villainous low.

Ste. Monster, lay-to your fingers : help to bear this
away, where my hogshead of wine is, or I'll turn you out
of my kingdom : Go to, carry this.[83]

Trin. And this.

Ste. Ay, and this.

*A noise of hunters heard. Enter divers Spirits in shape
of hounds, and hunt them about ;* PROSPERO *and* ARIEL
setting them on.

Pros. Hey, Mountain, hey !

Ari. Silver ! there it goes, Silver !

Pros. Fury, Fury ! there, Tyrant, there ! hark ! hark !—
          [CAL. STE. *and* TRIN. *are driven out.*
Go charge my goblins that they grind their joints
With dry convulsions ; shorten up their sinews
With aged cramps ; and more pinch-spotted make them
Than pard [84] or cat-o'-mountain.

Ari.   Hark, they roar !

Pros. Let them be hunted soundly.   At this hour
Lie at my mercy all mine enemies :
Shortly shall all my labours end, and thou
Shalt have the air at freedom : for a little
Follow, and do me service.   [*Exeunt.*

ACT V.   SCENE I.   *Before the Cell of* PROSPERO.

Enter PROSPERO *in his magic robes, and* ARIEL.

Pros. Now does my project gather to a head :
My charms crack not ; my spirits obey ; and Time
Goes upright with his carriage.   How's the day ?

[82] Caliban's barnacle is the *clakis* or *tree-goose*, as it was called, which
was thought to be produced from the shell-fish, *lepas antifera*, also called
barnacle. Gerard's *Herbal* has the following account of the matter : " There
are in the north parts of Scotland certain trees whereon do grow shell-
fishes, which, falling into the water, do become fowls, whom we call *bar-
nakles*, in the north of England *brant-geese*, and in Lancashire *tree-geese*."
Perhaps the old notion of the barnacle-goose being produced by the bar-
nacle-fish grew from the identity of name. As Caliban prides himself on
his intellectuality, he naturally has a horror of being turned into any thing
so stupid as a goose.

[83] The phrase *go to* occurs continually in the dramatic writers of Shakespeare's time. *Come on* and *hush up* are the senses in which it is most commonly used by the Poet.

[84] *Pard* was the common name for *leopard.*

Ari. On the sixth hour; at which time, my lord,
You said our work should cease.

Pros.   I did say so,
When first I rais'd the tempest.   Say, my spirit,
How fares the King and's followers?

Ari.   Confin'd together
In the same fashion as you gave in charge;
Just as you left them; all are prisoners, sir,
In the line-grove which weather-fends your cell;
They cannot budge till your release.[1]   The King,
His brother, and yours, abide all three distracted;
And the remainder mourning over them,
Brim-full of sorrow, and dismay; but chiefly
He that you term'd *The good old lord, Gonzalo:*
His tears run down his beard, like Winter's drops
From eaves of reeds: Your charm so strongly works 'em,
That, if you now beheld them, your affections
Would become tender.

Pros.   Dost thou think so, spirit?

Ari. Mine would, sir, were I human.

Pros.   And mine shall.
Hast thou, which art but air, a touch, a feeling
Of their afflictions, and shall not myself,
One of their kind, that relish all as sharply
Passion as they,[2] be kindlier mov'd than thou art?
Though with their high wrongs I am struck to th' quick,
Yet with my nobler reason 'gainst my fury
Do I take part: the rarer action is
In virtue than in vengeance: they being penitent,
The sole drift of my purpose doth extend
Not a frown further.   Go release them, Ariel:
My charms I'll break, their senses I'll restore,
And they shall be themselves.

Ari.   I'll fetch them, sir. [*Exit.*

Pros. Ye elves of hills, brooks, standing lakes, and
        groves;[3]
And ye that on the sands with printless foot
Do chase the ebbing Neptune, and do fly him

---

[1] Till you release them.   Another instance of the construction mentioned page 55, note 1. — *Weather-fends*, preceding line, is defends from the weather. — *Line-grove* is usually printed *lime-grove;* but line-tree is the true name of the tree referred to, and it stands so in the original.

[2] *All* is here used adverbially, in the sense of *quite;* and *passion* is the object of *relish*, and has the sense of *suffering.*   The sense of the passage is sometimes defeated by setting a comma after *sharply.*

[3] This speech is in some measure borrowed from Medea's, in *Ovid;* the expressions are, many of them, in the old translation by Golding.   But the exquisite fairy imagery is Shakespeare's own.

When he comes back; you demy-puppets that
By moon-shine do the green-sour ringlets make,[4]
Whereof the ewe not bites; and you whose pastime
Is to make midnight-mushrooms; that rejoice
To hear the solemn curfew;[5] by whose aid —
Weak masters though ye be[6] — I have be-dimm'd
The noon-tide Sun, call'd forth the mutinous winds,
And 'twixt the green sea and the azure vault
Set roaring war: to the dread rattling thunder
Have I given fire, and rifted Jove's stout oak
With his own bolt: the strong-bas'd promontory
Have I made shake, and by the spurs[7] pluck'd up
The pine and cedar: graves, at my command,
Have wak'd their sleepers, op'd, and let 'em forth,
By my so potent art. But this rough magic
I here abjure; and, when I have requir'd
Some heavenly music, — which even now I do, —
To work mine end upon their senses that
This airy charm is for, I'll break my staff,
Bury it certain fathoms in the earth,
And deeper than did ever plummet sound
I'll drown my book. *[Solemn Music.*

Re-enter ARIEL: *after him,* ALONSO, *with a frantic gesture, attended by* GONZALO; SEBASTIAN *and* ANTONIO
in like manner, attended by ADRIAN *and* FRANCISCO:
They all enter the circle which PROSPERO *had made,
and there stand charmed; which* PROSPERO *observing,
speaks.*

A solemn air, and the best comforter
To an unsettled fancy, cure thy brains,
Now useless, boil'd[8] within thy skull! — There stand,

---

[4] These *ringlets* were circles of bright-green grass, supposed to be produced by the footsteps of fairies dancing in a ring. The origin of them is
still, I believe, a mystery. They are alluded to in *A Midsummer-Night's
Dream,* ii. 1. — *Mushrooms* were also thought to be the work of fairies;
probably from their growing in rings, and springing up with such magical
quickness.

[5] They rejoice, because "the curfew tolls the knell of parting day," and
so signals the time for the fairies to begin their nocturnal frolics.

[6] *Weak,* if left to themselves, because they waste their force in sports and
in frivolous or discordant aims; but powerful when guided by wisdom, and
trained to worthy ends. This passage has often seemed to me a strange
prognostic of what human intelligence has since done in taming and
marshalling the great forces of Nature into the service of man.

[7] The *spurs* are the largest and longest roots of trees. The word is so used
again in *Cymbeline,* iv. 2.

[8] This seems to have been a common expression in reference to people
touched with madness, or with any passion that swamped their reason. So,
in *A Midsummer-Night's Dream,* v. 1: "Lovers and madmen have such
s.ething brains."

For you are spell-stopp'd. —
Holy Gonzalo, honourable man,
Mine eyes, even sociable to the show of thine,
Fall fellowly drops. — The charm dissolves apace ;
And as the morning steals upon the night,
Melting the darkness, so their rising senses
Begin to chase the ignorant fumes that mantle
Their clearer reason.[9] — O thou good Gonzalo,
My true preserver, and a loyal sir
To him thou follow'st! I will pay thy graces
Home both in word and deed. — Most cruelly
Didst thou, Alonso, use me and my daughter :
Thy brother was a furtherer in the act ; —
Thou'rt pinch'd for't now, Sebastian, flesh and blood. —
You, brother mine, that entertain'd ambition,
Expell'd remorse and nature ;[10] who, with Sebastian,
(Whose inward pinches therefore are most strong,)
Would here have kill'd your King ; I do forgive thee,
Unnatural though thou art! — Their understanding
Begins to swell ; and the approaching tide
Will shortly fill the reasonable shore,[11]
That now lies foul and muddy.   Not one of them
That yet looks on me, or would know me : — Ariel,
Fetch me the hat and rapier in my cell : —

[*Exit* ARIEL.

I will discase me, and myself present
As I was sometime Milan : — quickly, spirit :
Thou shalt ere long be free.

ARIEL *re-enters, singing, and helps to attire* PROSPERO.

Ari. Where the bee sucks, there suck I:
In a cowslip's bell I lie ;
There I couch when owls do cry :
On the bat's back I do fly
After Summer, merrily.[12]

[9] In this singular passage, *senses* means the *reason*, or the power of seeing things as they are.   So that the sense may be given something thus : their returning reason begins to dispel the blinding vapours that are gathered about it.

[10] *Remorse* is *pity, tenderness of heart ; nature* is *natural affection.*

[11] " The reasonable shore " is the shore of reason.

[12] " At night, ' when owls do cry,' Ariel couches ' in a cowslip's bell '; and he uses ' the bat's back ' as his pleasant vehicle, to pursue Summer in its progress round the world, and thus live merrily under continual blossoms."   Such appears the most natural as well as most poetical meaning of this much disputed passage.   As a matter of fact, however, bats do not migrate in quest of Summer, but become torpid in winter.   Was the Poet ignorant of this, or did he disregard it, thinking that such beings as Ariel were not bound to observe the rules of natural history?

Merrily, merrily, shall I live now,
Under the blossom that hangs on the bough.

Pros. Why, that's my dainty Ariel! I shall miss thee;
But yet thou shalt have freedom: — so, so, so. —
To the King's ship, invisible as thou art:
There shalt thou find the mariners asleep
Under the hatches; the master and the boatswain
Being awake, enforce them to this place,
And presently, I pr'ythee.

   Ari. I drink the air before me, and return
Or e'er your pulse twice beat.　　　　　[*Exit* ARIEL.

   Gon. All torment, trouble, wonder, and amazement
Inhabit here: some heavenly power guide us
Out of this fearful country!

   Pros.　　　　　　　Behold, Sir King,
The wronged Duke of Milan, Prospero:
For more assurance that a living prince
Does now speak to thee, I embrace thy body;
And to thee and thy company I bid
A hearty welcome.

   Alon.　　　　　　Whe'r thou beest he or no,
Or some enchanted [13] trifle to abuse me,
As late I have been, I not know: thy pulse
Beats, as of flesh and blood; and, since I saw thee,
Th' affliction of my mind amends, with which,
I fear, a madness held me: this must crave
(An if this be at all) a most strange story.
Thy dukedom I resign; and do entreat
Thou pardon me my wrongs.[14]　But how should Prospero
Be living and be here?

   Pros.　　　　　　First, noble friend,
Let me embrace thine age, whose honour cannot
Be measur'd or confin'd.

   Gon.　　　　　　Whether this be
Or be not, I'll not swear.

   Pros.　　　　　　You do yet taste
Some subtilties [15] o' the isle, that will not let you
Believe things certain. — Welcome, my friends all: —

---

[13] *Enchanted* for *enchanting*, or having the power of enchantment. This undifferentiated use of the active and passive forms has been repeatedly noted. See vol. i. page 139, note 16, and page 66, note 4. Walker, however, thinks the meaning to be, "*some trifle produced by enchantment to abuse me.*"

[14] Still another instance of the construction mentioned in note 2 of this scene. "*My* wrongs" may mean either the wrongs I have *done*, or the wrongs I have *suffered.* Here it means the former.

[15] *Subtilties* are quaint deceptive inventions; the word is common to ancient cookery, in which a disguised or ornamented dish is so termed.

[*Aside to* Seb. *and* Ant.] But you, my brace of lords,
      were I so minded,
I here could pluck his Highness' frown upon you,
And justify you traitors: [16] at this time
I'll tell no tales.
    Seb. [*Aside.*] The Devil speaks in him.
    Pros.   No. —
For you, most wicked sir, whom to call brother
Would even infect my mouth, I do forgive
Thy rankest faults, — all of them; and require
My dukedom of thee, which perforce, I know,
Thou must restore.
    Alon.   If thou be'st Prospero,
Give us particulars of thy preservation;
How thou hast met us here, who three hours since
Were wreck'd upon this shore; where I have lost —
How sharp the point of this remembrance is! —
My dear son Ferdinand.
    Pros.   I'm woe for't, sir.
    Alon. Irreparable is the loss; and Patience
Says it is past her cure.
    Pros.   I rather think
You have not sought her help; of whose soft grace,
For the like loss I have her sovereign aid,
And rest myself content.
    Alon.   You the like loss!
    Pros. As great to me as late; and, supportable
To make the dear loss, have I means much weaker
Than you may call to comfort you; for I
Have lost my daughter.
    Alon.   A daughter!
O Heavens, that they were living both in Naples,
The King and Queen there! that they were, I wish
Myself were mudded in that oozy bed
Where my son lies. When did you lose your daughter?
    Pros. In this last tempest. I perceive, these lords
At this encounter do so much admire,
That they devour their reason, and scarce think
Their eyes do offices of truth, their words
Are natural breath: but, howsoe'er you have
Been justled from your senses, know for certain
That I am Prospero, and that very Duke
Which was thrust forth of Milan; who most strangely
Upon this shore, where you were wreck'd, was landed,
To be the lord on't. No more yet of this;

---

16 *Prove* you traitors, or justify myself for calling you such.

For 'tis a chronicle of day by day,
Not a relation for a breakfast, nor
Befitting this first meeting.   Welcome, sir;
This cell's my court : here have I few attendants,
And subjects none abroad : pray you, look in.
My dukedom since you've given me again,
I will requite you with as good a thing;
At least bring forth a wonder to content ye
As much as me my dukedom.

The entrance of the Cell opens, and discovers FERDINAND
and MIRANDA *playing at chess.*

Mira. Sweet lord, you play me false.
Ferd.   No, my dear'st love,
I would not for the world.
Mira. Yes, for a score of kingdoms you should wrangle,
And I would call it fair play.
Alon.   If this prove
A vision of the island, one dear son
Shall I twice lose.[17]
Seb.   A most high miracle !
Ferd. Though the seas threaten, they are merciful!
I've curs'd them without cause.   [*Kneels to* ALON.
Alon.   Now all the blessings
Of a glad father compass thee about !
Arise, and say how thou cam'st here.
Mira.   O, wonder !
How many goodly creatures are there here !
How beauteous mankind is !   O brave new world,
That has such people in't !
Pros.   'Tis new to thee.
Alon. What is this maid with whom thou wast at play ?
Your eld'st acquaintance cannot be three hours :
Is she the goddess that hath sever'd us,
And brought us thus together ?
Ferd.   Sir, she's mortal ;
But by immortal Providence she's mine :
I chose her when I could not ask my father
For his advice, nor thought I had one.   She
Is daughter to this famous Duke of Milan,
Of whom so often I have heard renown,
But never saw before ; of whom I have
Receiv'd a second life ; and second father
This lady makes him to me.

[17] He has lost him once in supposing him drowned, and will lose him a
second time when the vision is dispelled.

Alon.   I am hers:
But, O, how oddly will it sound that I
Must ask my child forgiveness!
   Pros.   There, sir, stop:
Let us not burden our remembrance with
A heaviness that's gone.
   Gon.   I've inly wept,
Or should have spoke ere this. — Look down, you gods,
And on this couple drop a blessed crown!
For it is you that have chalk'd forth the way
Which brought us hither.
   Alon.   I say, Amen, Gonzalo!
   Gon. Was Milan thrust from Milan, that his issue
Should become Kings of Naples?   O, rejoice
Beyond a common joy! and set it down
With gold on lasting pillars: In one voyage
Did Claribel her husband find at Tunis;
And Ferdinand, her brother, found a wife
Where he himself was lost; Prospero, his dukedom,
In a poor isle; and all of us, ourselves,
When no man was his own.[18]
   Alon. [*To* FERD. *and* MIRA.] Give me your hands:
Let grief and sorrow still embrace his heart
That doth not wish you joy!
   Gon.   Be't so! Amen! —

Re-enter ARIEL, *with the Master and Boatswain amaz-
edly following.*

O, look, sir, look, sir! here is more of us.
I prophesied, if a gallows were on land,
This fellow could not drown. — Now, blasphemy,
That swear'st grace o'erboard, not an oath on shore?
Hast thou no mouth by land?   What is the news?
   Boats. The best news is, that we have safely found
Our King and company; the next, our ship —
Which, but three glasses since, we gave out split —
Is tight, and yare, and bravely rigg'd, as when
We first put out to sea.
   Ari. [*Aside to* PROS.] Sir, all this service
Have I done since I went.
   Pros. [*Aside to* ARI.] My tricksy spirit!
   Alon. These are not natural events; they strengthen
From strange to stranger. — Say, how came you hither?
   Boats. If I did think, sir, I were well awake,
I'd strive to tell you.   We were dead of sleep,

[18] When no man was *in his senses*, or had *self-possession.*

And — how we know not — all clapp'd under hatches;
Where, but even now, with strange and several noises
Of roaring, shrieking, howling, jingling chains,
And more diversity of sounds, all horrible,
We were awak'd; straightway, at liberty:
When we, in all her trim, freshly beheld
Our royal, good, and gallant ship; our master
Capering to eye her: on a trice, so please you,
Even in a dream, were we divided from them,　　＼
And were brought moping hither.
  Ari. [*Aside to* Pros.]   Was't well done?
  Pros. [*Aside to* Ari.] Bravely, my diligence. Thou
    shalt be free.
  Alon. This is as strange a maze as e'er men trod;
And there is in this business more than Nature
Was ever conduct of: some oracle
Must rectify our knowledge.
  Pros.   Sir, my liege,
Do not infest your mind with beating on [19]
The strangeness of this business; at pick'd leisure,
Which shall be shortly, single I'll resolve you [20] —
Which to you shall seem probable — of every
These happen'd accidents: till when, be cheerful,
And think of each thing well. — [*Aside to* Ari.] Come
    hither, spirit:
Set Caliban and his companions free;
Untie the spell. [*Exit* Ariel.] — How fares my gracious
    sir?
There are yet missing of your company
Some few odd lads that you remember not.

  Re-enter Ariel, *driving in* Caliban, Stephano, *and*
    Trinculo, *in their stolen Apparel.*

  Ste. Every man shift for all the rest,[21] and let no man
take care for himself; for all is but fortune. — Coragio,
bully-monster, coragio!
  Trin. If these be true spies which I wear in my head,
here's a goodly sight.
  Cal. O Setebos, these be brave spirits indeed!
How fine my master is! I am afraid
He'll chástise me.

  [19] There is an expression still in use, of similar import: "Still *hammering*
at it."
  [20] *Resolve* was much used for *inform* or *assure.* See vol. i. page 481,
note 14.
  [21] Stephano's tongue is rather tipsy still, and here staggers into a mis-
placement of his words: he means, Let every man shift for himself.

Seb. Ha, ha!
What things are these, my lord Antonio?
Will money buy 'em?

Ant.   Very like; one of them
Is a plain fish, and, no doubt, marketable.

Pros. Mark but the badges of these men, my lords,
Then say if they be true. This mis-shap'd knave,—
His mother was a witch; and one so strong
That could control the Moon, make flows and ebbs,
And deal in her command, without her power.[22]
These three have robb'd me; and this demi-devil
(For he's a bastard one) had plotted with them
To take my life: two of these fellows you
Must know and own; this thing of darkness I
Acknowledge mine.

Cal.   I shall be pinch'd to death.

Alon. Is not this Stephano, my drunken butler?

Seb. He is drunk now: where had he wine?

Alon. And Trinculo is reeling ripe: where should they
Find this grand liquor that hath gilded 'em? [23] —
How cam'st thou in this pickle?

Trin. I have been in such a pickle, since I saw you last,
that, I fear me, will never out of my bones: I shall not
fear fly-blowing.

Seb. Why, how now, Stephano!

Ste. O, touch me not! I am not Stephano, but a
cramp.

Pros. You'd be King o' the isle, sirrah?

Ste. I should have been a sore one, then.

Alon. [*Pointing to* CAL.] This is as strange a thing as
    e'er I look'd on.

Pros. He is as disproportion'd in his manners
As in his shape. — Go, sirrah, to my cell;
Take with you your companions; as you look
To have my pardon, trim it handsomely.

Cal. Ay, that I will; and I'll be wise hereafter,
And seek for grace. What a thrice double ass
Was I, to take this drunkard for a god,
And worship this dull fool!

Pros.   Go to; away!

Alon. Hence, and bestow your luggage where you
    found it.

---

[22] The Moon seems to be here regarded as having the power to cause
"flows and ebbs"; while Sycorax, though without that power, could *command* them, whether the Moon would or no. Not far, perhaps, from being
"a distinction without a difference."

[23] The phrase of being *gilded* was a trite one for being *drunk.*

Seb. Or stole it, rather. [*Exeunt* CAL., STE., *and* TRIN.
Pros. Sir, I invite your Highness and your train
To my poor cell, where you shall take your rest
For this one night; which, part of it, I'll waste
With such discourse as, I not doubt, shall make it
Go quick away, — the story of my life,
And the particular accidents gone by,
Since I came to this isle: and in the morn
I'll bring you to your ship, and so to Naples,
Where I have hope to see the nuptial
Of these our dear-beloved solemniz'd;
And thence retire me to my Milan, where
Every third thought shall be my grave.
   Alon.   I long
To hear the story of your life, which must
Take the ear strangely.
   Pros.   I'll deliver all;
And promise you calm seas, auspicious gales,
And sail so expeditious, that shall catch
Your royal fleet far off. — [*Aside to* ARI.] My Ariel, —
     chick, —
That is thy charge: then to the elements
Be free, and fare thou well! — Please you, draw near.
                                 [*Exeunt.*

EPILOGUE.

SPOKEN BY PROSPERO.

Now my charms are all o'erthrown,
And what strength I have's mine own, —
Which is most faint: now, 'tis true,
I must be here confin'd by you,
Or sent to Naples. Let me not,
Since I have my dukedom got,
And pardon'd the deceiver, dwell
In this bare island by your spell;
But release me from my bands,
With the help of your good hands.[24]
Gentle breath of yours my sails

[24] The Epilogue is supposed to be addressed to the audience, and the speaker here solicits their applause by the clapping of their hands. Noise was supposed to dissolve a spell; hence the applause would release him from his bands. See page 59, note 18.

Must fill, or else my project fails,
Which was to please : now I want
Spirits to enforce, art to enchant;
And my ending is despair,
Unless I be reliev'd by prayer;
Which pierces so, that it assaults
Mercy itself, and frees all faults.
As you from crimes would pardon'd be,
Let your indulgence set me free.[25]

[25] Mr. White expresses a confident opinion that this Epilogue is not of Shakespeare's writing. It has long seemed to me to have quite another texture and grain than the Poet's undoubted workmanship; and I am glad to have my own sense of the matter confirmed by so competent a judgment. Mr. White justly observes that such appendages were very apt to be written by some second hand; and in Shakespeare's circle of friends and fellow-dramatists there were more than one who might well have done this office for him, either with or without his consent; especially as his plays are known to have passed out of his hands into the keeping of the theatrical company for which he wrote. Both the Prologue and the Epilogue of *King Henry VIII.* have been noted by Johnson and others as decidedly wanting in the right Shakespearian taste. See, also, vol. i. page 426, note 6.